I0822436

ENDORSEMENTS

"Life After E.L.E. left me dumbstruck . . . and happy and sad and excited and weepy and a little bit in love. It's very Hunger Games meets The Day After Tomorrow. If you are looking for an exciting fast-paced read, this is the story for you!"

~ **Julie Hall,** *USA Today* Bestselling author of the ***Life After*** series

"Life After E.L.E. is a post apocalyptic dystopian that will keep you turning the pages. J.C. Morrows is a must-read author!"

~ **Mandy Fender,** Award winning author of the ***Defier*** series

"A strong heroine braves the frigid wastes of a dead world in Life After E.L.E. This dystopian's tyrannical government, lovable characters, and struggle for survival will leave you itching for the next book."

~ **Jamie Foley,** author of ***The Sentinel*** trilogy

"JC Morrows grabs your attention on the first page and doesn't let go until you come to the end. All her books leave you wanting and ready to read the next in the series. Enjoy!"

~ **Toni Shiloh,** author of ***Buying Love***

"Engaging and full of suspense, JC's work keeps me on the edge of my seat ... from the first paragraph, I found myself unable to put down the story until the very last word."

~ **Naomi Miller** , author of the ***Amish Sweet Shop Mystery*** series

"JC Morrows builds suspense and an ominous setting that will leave you eager to read more of her MoonStone series."

~ **A. J. Cattapan** , author of the YA novel ***Angelhood***

BOOKS BY JC MORROWS

Order of the MoonStone series

A Reluctant Assassin

A Treacherous Decision

A Desperate Escape

A Tragic Consequence

A Broken Kingdom

Short Stories and Novellas

A Perilous Assignment

A Cunning Masquerade

A Dangerous Love

A Covert Alliance

A Mysterious Masque

Frozen World series

LIFE AFTER E.L.E.

Coming Soon

ESCAPE AFTER E.L.E.

Life after E.L.E.

Life after E.L.E.

FROZEN WORLD - PART ONE

JC MORROWS

Life After E.L.E.

Mystic Moonstone Press, Knoxville, TN
www.mysticmoonstonepress.wordpress.com

ISBN: 978-0692669044 (Trade Paperback)
ISBN: 978-1948733410 (Hardbound)
ASIN: B01LWY1XP4 (Kindle)

1. Teen Fiction / Post-Apocalyptic. 2. Teen Fiction / Dystopian. 3. Teen Fiction / Action & Adventure / Survival Stories. 4. Teen Fiction / Clean Read.

For everyone who got me
through that first
NaNoWriMo!

A NOTE FROM THE AUTHOR

Hi there beloved reader.

Whether you have read my Order of the MoonStone series—or *Life After E.L.E.* is the first book of mine that you've picked up, I just want to take a moment to say thank you.

I wrote this story three years ago on a whim. Honestly, I never *really* expected it to be published. If it were not for the sheer number of people who were so excited about the story idea, you likely would not be holding it in your hands right now.

And I already have readers touting it as the best thing I've written so far. . .

I can only hope you will agree.

ENJOY!

~ JC

PROLOGUE

Outside the Arizona Caves

Year 45 A.E.

Day 171

The muscles in my legs were screaming from over-use, burning with exhaustion. . . but I knew I couldn't stop. . . I could not rest. To stop or even to slow down would mean death.

If I didn't get to the gates in time, if I didn't make it, I would be locked out.

They would close them, lock them and it would be too late. They didn't wait for anyone.

I knew this better than most.

I had watched, screaming, while my father had been locked out. I had screamed and cried and begged until someone had to drag me away to the infirmary.

I had fought them all the way.

I had struggled and scratched and even bit at those who were pulling me away, trying desperately to get free, to see him again, to call out to him over the walls, to tell him I loved him one last time, because I knew I would never see him again.

No one survived on the outside—not overnight.

It was the first rule we all learned. Some learned it the hard way. You were either in the compound by sunset or you were dead.

Now I was on the outside—and I was out of time.

So I ran.

I pushed my over-taxed muscles even harder. I could already hear the sound of the heavy wheels that moved the doors into place.

And I knew—I knew I was not going to make it. . .

ONE

Arizona Caves

Year 45 A.E.

Day 79

I woke to alarms screaming. There were bright red and yellow lights flashing above the doorway of the small, round hatch that lead into the hallway that led to our common room.

Without even being completely awake, my body knew what to do. My feet hit the cold floor, toes searching for the edges of my boots. Only when my searching toes didn't find them, did I start to really wake up.

It didn't matter if this was a drill or not. I would be in big trouble if I didn't get out in time.

I forced my eyes open and looked around in the half-light, trying to make my eyes acclimate quickly. After precious moments that I really couldn't afford, my eyes began to adjust and I finally spotted my boots at the foot of my bed. Someone had knocked them over. I reached over, grabbed them, pulling them on roughly—in a real hurry now.

I looked down at my pajamas. They were not my oldest pair so they would probably be fine for a drill. But what if it wasn't a drill. . .

Oh well. If it isn't a drill, it will hardly matter what I'm wearing.

Pushing up out of my bed, I was almost running as I went through the doorway.

Stop worrying. It's just a drill. It has to be a drill. . . right?

I told myself this every time I was awakened in the middle of the night by one of these emergency drills. Thus far, they had all been just another drill.

But one day. . .

With that in mind, I grabbed my heavy coat as I went by the hooks on the wall—just in case. Then I skidded to a stop just as my grandmother stepped through her own hatch beside me.

"Is everything all right, Eve?"

There was a look of concern in her eyes as she asked; she knew there was something unusual going on. I was normally the first one out of our unit during a drill. And now I was dragging so far behind that I was almost the last one to leave.

I still felt like I was half asleep, but I knew I had to reassure her. "It's fine, Gran. Couldn't find my boots is all."

My answer must have satisfied her because she nodded her head and turned to move through the main room with no further comment. I followed quickly, noting the light on by Dad's chair as I moved through the main room.

Mom must have been working late again. Grandad was probably sitting up again, reading.

Mom had worked the late shift for weeks—which was odd. Typically someone only worked the night shift once a month, or even once every few months. As a rule, every person within a division took turns with late shifts so that no one had to do more than their fair share.

The rest of the family was either moving through the hatch or already taking their place in line with the rest of our unit when I caught up. A couple of our neighbors looked surprised to see me in the back of my family line.

Is it really such a shock to everyone that I took longer than the rest of the family just once?

It was a struggle to school my face back into a blank look and wipe the anger off my features.

Once! It's just one time. Why does everyone have to make such a big deal about it?

And then—before I could dwell on it any longer—we were moving. We followed the people in front of us and they followed the people in front of them until we filed out the main doors of our section.

As we moved out into the main hall, I shrugged into my coat, but didn't zip it up yet. The warmth would be needed soon enough, but it would not be a good idea to start sweating before we got outside. The dangers of being sweaty and going outdoors was something we were taught as tiny children.

Everyone moved quickly to the main entryway. As my family passed through the large metal opening, I pulled my hood up over my head, zipping my coat to keep warm, as I followed them outside. A glance at the digital on my wrist told me that it was 2 A.M.; which meant it would still be well into the negative temps—even within the safety of the gates.

I wished momentarily that I had put on my flannel pajamas—instead of the soft cotton ones—last night before going to bed, but the cotton pajamas were my favorites. I loved the feel of the soft fabric against my skin, so I wore them more often than the flannel ones.

I also knew there was no point in lamenting it at this point. There wasn't anything I could do about it now.

As the other sections filed out, I noticed a small group of people that were being led out by the guards. A tiny gasp escaped my lips before I could catch it, when I recognized one of the faces.

I clamped my lips shut and prayed no one had heard it. I didn't want anyone to have a reason to accuse me of being a conspirator, but my eyes didn't leave her face. I didn't know her name, but I knew she was a neighbor. I could remember seeing her face in the circle of young people that gathered around my grandparents; who sometimes told stories in the evenings.

There was a large bruise on her cheek, dried blood on her lower lip and a look of absolute terror in her eyes. They were open wider than normal and she kept looking around, with little jerky movements.

Someone standing next to her put their arm around her and she seemed to relax a little, but the question remained in my mind—what was she doing in that group? What had this group of young people done to deserve such a punishment? There was only one reason we would all be out here in the bitter cold —only one reason the guards would be surrounding the little group of people.

The only reason the gates were ever opened after the evening bell rang. . .

Someone had committed a terrible crime; something that was

bad enough to warrant a death sentence—because being outside the compound on your own after dark meant death. We all knew that. It was much too cold, especially at two in the morning.

No one could survive out there for more than a few minutes in such cold. It was the first rule we all learned.

It was then that I looked—really looked—at their clothes, almost as if the thought of how terribly cold it must be was what brought them to mind.

Only a few of them were wearing coats.

I could even see one person with no shoes, and as my eyes traveled up his thin form, I noticed there was also no coat on his adolescent body. When my searching eyes finally reached his face, I saw that he was a very young man—and even though I thought I could see a hint of fear in his eyes, he stood straight and there was a proud lift to his chin.

There were also fresh bruises on his cheek and a thick white bandage on his forehead.

Well at least they bandaged his wound. The thought soured as it passed through my mind, but I forced myself to let it go. It would be worse for them, as well as me, if anyone else was drawn into their punishment now—standing in front of the whole compound.

As I glanced back at the young man, I forced a bland,

expressionless look onto my face. He was surrounded by others who had the same proud lift and ramrod-straight stance.

They were obviously frightened, but they were doing everything they could to look unafraid. Even as I forced myself not to show emotion, I felt admiration for them rise in me. Here they were—about to be shoved out to certain death, yet they were showing nothing, but strength and unity.

As I looked around the group, I saw others with fresh cuts and bruises; not all of them were bandaged, either. One small boy had a splint on his arm. I looked at him more closely. He couldn't be more than ten, but he was standing there with the same stiff posture and a pride so strong, it was bordering on arrogance. There was also a fiery defiance in his eyes, but I could see slightly dirty tracks running down his cheeks that looked like they might have been made by tears.

Thoughts were rushing through my head; memories of things my father had told me were piling up so fast I couldn't seem to hold onto any of them.

I tried to think of what this group of young people could possibly have done that warranted death. There wasn't even one adult in the group. A couple of them looked like they were close, but they were definitely all apprentice age or even younger.

Had no one taken that into consideration? Surely they were

led by an adult. Where was that person? Shouldn't their punishment be just as severe? Or worse?

My thoughts were interrupted by the harsh sound of the chancellor's voice. He was speaking to the entire group, but his words sounded like they were aimed at one person.

"You have one final chance. Will you yield?" He was looking hard at one person in the group, but I couldn't tell who it was from my vantage point.

He let his words hang there, while he kept his hard eyes trained on someone in the group before him. As time stretched out immeasurably, I found myself silently urging someone to step forward; to take responsibility for these young people.

Why would any adult worth their skin—leave this group of kids to hang for them? Why wouldn't they just step forward?

Why don't the kids rat him out? Surely they know who they're working for.

But the silence reigned. No one stepped forward and not one person in the group said a word.

After what felt like an eternity, the chancellor broke contact with a jerk of his head and looked around at all those in the little group. I watched as each one stiffened and realized it must be while the chancellor's glance was directly on them. Several of them pursed their lips tightly, too. Obviously, they weren't going to do whatever he wanted of them. And we all knew what that would mean.

I turned as I heard the dull clang of the enormous evening bell and then the sound of the gate mechanisms moving as they slowly opened inward.

A strong gust of wind blew in through the tiny opening, bringing a whirlwind of snow and cold air into the square. I heard a slight shuffle behind me and looked to my right to see everyone around me pulling their coats tighter around their bodies. I started to do the same until the thought of those young people who were about to be sent out into that cold and snow without coats. . . and the one boy who wore no shoes. And it made me feel ashamed.

I fleetingly wondered if I could give my coat to one of them. . . the young boy, perhaps.

Will they even let me do that? Or would it look like I was one of them? I quickly realized how silly it was to even think such a thing. It couldn't possibly do any good—even if they would let me.

I never got a chance to do more than wonder about it, because the group was moving toward the gates.

As I watched them, it occurred to me that the guards were not pushing or struggling with anyone. The little group of young people was moving toward the gates freely—still with their backs straight and heads held high.

It shocked me to realize there were tears running down my face. I dashed them away quickly, before anyone else could notice, then I looked back at the group, as they reached the enormous gates.

All I could see now were their backs, as they steadily moved forward. They were struggling now, but it wasn't against the guards; it was against the strong winds that were swirling fiercely in through the half-opened gates. As they moved forward, the guards moved into a line behind them, but they didn't follow beyond the gates.

As the last person was swallowed up by the mass of white, the gate mechanisms started moving again. There was a quickly muffled cry from somewhere behind us, but I didn't dare turn to look—although several of the people in front of me did.

I didn't take my eyes off the gates as they closed. The scream of the strong winds and the rumble of the heavy doors moving had brought a familiar memory crashing back to my mind.

TWO

Arizona Caves

Year 40 A.E.

Day 221

Mother had sent me to deliver Grandfather's dinner. I'd had to go up into the watchtower and ended up waiting there with him, because his replacement had not yet arrived. We were sitting there talking when we'd both been startled by a distant shout and we'd turned to see where it had come from.

My heart felt like it stopped when I saw a figure struggling through the snow, heading for the gates as quickly as the thick drifts would allow. It took only a second to realize that he couldn't possibly make it in time. The gates were almost closed and he was still so far away.

I jumped down to run along the wall, thinking surely the gate operator must not be able to see the man out there; struggling to reach them before they closed. I got halfway to the gate tower before Grandfather caught me and pulled me back. I struggled against him, but the arms that had always held me so gently were suddenly like iron around my thrashing body.

I cried out, but he shushed me and started trying to pull me back to his tower post. As I struggled in his arms, the figure got a little closer and my struggles stopped for just a moment —and then started again with a renewed strength when I realized that the man's face was all too familiar.

I would remember later, but at the time I didn't realize the screams I could hear were coming from my own throat. And I couldn't hear the voice in my ear clearly; the voice was muffled by my own screams and the pounding of my heart.

I struggled and screamed as the gates closed and then I could only watch as my father stood there in snow that was almost up to his knees.

Clearly, he knew he wasn't going to make it—and he'd stopped fighting his way forward.

For a moment, all of my struggles and screams stopped. As I locked eyes with him, he looked up. I could see his face so much more clearly now, even through the tears that were streaming down my face.

We stood there—looking at each other for what felt like an eternity, before I saw him shake his head slightly and smile up at me. Then he turned and headed back toward the towering trees.

And that was it.

That was the last time I had seen my father.

I knew the rules; everyone knew the rules. They were taught to us almost from the day we could walk. The first rule everyone learned was to be inside the gates before dark, because once they were closed for the night, it was too late.

At the time, I had been so sure that an exception would be made with someone so close, especially someone as important as my dad—someone who worked in the chancellor's office. My father was an important man.

That should have made a difference.

But it hadn't.

The gates had closed and Grandfather's replacement had arrived during my struggles. I remember vaguely that it was Grandfather who had taken me down to the infirmary. By the time we reached it, I was inconsolable. My screams had finally quieted, but the sobs that had torn through my tiny body had been so strong, I'd had trouble breathing.

I didn't remember much after that. Either I had blacked out from a lack of air or they'd given me something that knocked me out—pretty quickly.

Either way, the next thing I remembered was waking up in my own bed.

THREE

Arizona Caves

Year 45 A.E.

Day 79

The final thud of the enormous gates closing brought my attention back to the present. The people in front of me had stopped looking behind them. Everyone was facing the chancellor as he walked back and forth in front of us.

The look on his face was so fierce it was almost frightening, but for some reason it did not even faze me. When I thought about it, I realized I had long ago seen the very worst of him, so it made perfect sense that he didn't scare me anymore.

I watched with an odd detachment as he walked back and forth, his boot heels making hollow clangs on the hard ground under his feet. As he moved across the raised platform in front of us, he looked angrier than I had seen him in a very long time.

The group of young people—that had just suffered the harshest punishment that could be imposed—must have done something that had really gotten under his skin. I struggled to control the laughter that was bubbling up in my chest along with a sudden and irrational desire to smile.

I knew it would be a very bad idea to give away how it thrilled me to see him thwarted. . . and by kids no less. . . so I struggled to keep my features calm and blank; even forcing myself to look less alert than I felt.

It had been a long time since someone in the caves had done something heinous enough to warrant such a severe punishment. And I could not remember a time when so many had been punished all at once.

I risked taking a quick look at the few buildings we had been able to add on to the cave complex, since the chancellor kept glancing in that direction himself, but there was no obvious, visible damage. Perhaps if there was damage, it had been done on the inside.

Either way, those things had a way of making the rounds in the caves and I felt certain we would all hear about it sometime soon, so I looked back at the chancellor. He was still pacing back and forth in front of the group of us and his expression might have actually become fiercer.

He's certainly in rare form tonight.

Some of the people around me began to shift uncomfortably. Apparently most people had thought this would be another drill so, like me, they hadn't put on their thick outdoor clothes. Maybe some of them had even forgotten to put on their heavy thermal coats, which made me glad I had thought to do so. . . especially since the chancellor showed no signs of being in a hurry to let us get back to our nice warm beds.

It was a struggle, but I did my best to stand still, knowing it was never a good idea to get his attention when he was in such a mood.

Thinking about the people around me who were obviously cold, my thoughts turned back to the people who were outside the gate now.

Were they heading for the forest? Would they be able to navigate through the strong winds and deep snow?

How long will the ones without adequate protection be able to last in this intense cold?

Will their companions try to help them? I truly hoped they would. They had certainly presented a united front earlier.

I hope they won't just leave them behind—knowing the situation is probably hopeless—and try instead to just look after themselves?

And then of course, my mind kept coming back to the most obvious question.

What could they have done to deserve such a punishment?

I was jerked from my line of thought by the sound of the chancellor's voice and even I could not help but notice the unusually deep gravel of his tone.

"What you have just witnessed was not justice." The words came out clipped and harsh.

He must really be struggling with his temper. What could those kids have done—to warrant such anger?

"However, it was the most severe punishment I could have dealt those criminals." He had been pacing as he spoke, but now he stopped and turned to face us.

"I want to make myself perfectly clear. We cannot afford to harbor criminals here. Their activities. . ." He stopped for a moment, gesturing to the buildings behind him, ". . . threaten us all. They must be dealt with swiftly or we will all pay the consequences."

He stood very still, but his eyes were searching the crowd, almost as if he was looking for another criminal hiding among them.

"If anyone has information about a criminal, it is their duty to come forward. I cannot stress this enough." He turned and looked behind him at the gate—and then back at the crowd.

"The consequences of allowing those who would cause us harm—to stay here—affect us all. Such behavior will be treated as treason. We must all do our part to keep the peace here."

He turned his head to look all around the crowd that surrounded me, his eyes seeming to pin each one of us for at least a second. "The alternative is death for all of us."

And it could have been my imagination, but it seemed like he looked at some people longer than the rest. It might have been a sign that he suspected them, or it might have just been an attempt to intimidate everyone enough that the guilty parties would accidentally incriminate themselves.

Then, without warning, he turned and strode back to the complex. The crowd parted before him, people scrambling out of his way as he stormed through.

Once he was inside, we all looked around at each other for a moment, before following at a slightly slower pace; automatically falling back into the lines we had formed to file outside.

I listened to the conversations around me as I waited for the people in front of me to move forward. The hushed conversations ran the gamut from speculation about who else might be involved to what the punishment might be for someone hiding criminal activity.

No one else seemed concerned that the chancellor's

punishment might have been too harsh or that the "criminals" he had just sentenced to death were children. And that got me thinking.

Why is no one concerned, bothered, or outraged at what just happened? The chancellor just sentenced a group of children to death.

What was worse, he'd done it in such a nasty way that my stomach was still churning, just thinking about it.

When did we all become so callous?

Looking around me at the people I had grown up with, I suddenly felt as if I was seeing things through new eyes.

I mean obviously there was nothing that could be done about it, but why did we all just accept it as inevitable and miss the tyranny of such a move?

That made me think about the high government and what they might have thought about all of this. *If only we had not lost contact with the moon base all those years ago. . .*

It wasn't exactly common knowledge, but I knew they should really be the ones in charge. They would be the ones responsible for making the big decisions, passing laws, and handing out punishments.

If they were still around. . .

I could not remember a time when even one person was punished so harshly—much less an entire group, and certainly never the children.

Of course it doesn't really count as punishment for those who are caught outside after time for the gate to close. . . does it?

I had to wonder if the chancellor had come up with this punishment himself. He was a hard man, but this. . . this would make him a monster! Could this have been a sentence he was forced to hand down because of his position? If so, why now?

Never could I remember this happening before.

Even without the high government—there must be laws written down somewhere.

Could it be that the chancellor is only enforcing those laws? Could he really be just as much an innocent bystander as we all are?

FOUR

Arizona Caves

Year 45 A.E.

Day 81

I woke to the normal sounds of morning, which had me scrambling out of bed. I was almost always up for an hour or more before the early morning klaxon.

Why did I stay up so late reading those old notebooks of Dad's. . . again? There's nothing in them.

What was I hoping to find?

I already know more history than almost anyone else in this place, thanks to Dad. . . and Grandad.

Almost no one from my generation knew anything about the

old world, from the time before the caves. . . before the extinction level event that had forced us all underground. . . the time before extinction had been a very real possibility.

Hardly anyone spoke of it. The majority of the original group who had built our little sanctuary were long gone by now.

Grandad remembered; he and Grandmother, but she never spoke of that time, and the small number of books that were brought with the original colonists had been locked away long ago because they were crumbling—so there was no real way the younger generation could know anything about it all. . . unless some of their grandparents shared stories with them, as well.

Like my grandparents. . . *well, like Grandad, anyway.*

Grandad is a wonderful storyteller. He tells me about his job before the caves. It sounds interesting, but sometimes I get the feeling that he embellishes. . . at least a little. I am certain all the things from their stories could not possibly be real.

I'm pretty sure there's no one except me who even knows what a climatologist is. . . or what it was, anyway.

His stories are full of crazy words like hothouse gasses and global warming. He says all the time how his fellow scientists were so sure the Earth was headed for exactly the kind of disaster we've been through, but no one thought it would be because of a moon attracted to our sun's gravity.

He says some of them even said it was a good thing the moon hit us first; they were sure we were headed for worse.

I get the feeling he doesn't really think they were right, though. I'm not sure why—because he never says that. He just has this look on his face when he says it. . . it makes me think he's laughing at them. . . on the inside.

My grandmother doesn't have quite as many stories. She was an aide to some big government official.

I forget who.

She doesn't like to talk about him much. I think it's because he didn't make it to the caves in time. But I'm not really sure that's all there is to it. She says things here would be a lot better if he were here.

Grandad always looks a little upset when she starts talking about him. I think he must be one of the secrets I'm not supposed to tell anyone else.

I'm one of the lucky ones. I know that. My grandparents both made it into the colony with my mother. They were considered essential personnel so they were guaranteed a place in the caves.

They tell the children stories in the evening. Sometimes adults even wander over from their evening tasks to listen.

Sometimes, there are even things they tell me that they don't tell anyone else.

Of course these things they tell me only within the walls of our little home and they always make a point of telling me that they're not to be passed on to anyone else.

Fortunately, I am no stranger to secrets.

I've had secrets for years, since before my father died. It might not always be easy to keep them, but I learned as a very young child that some secrets can be dangerous—so that helps me to remember.

At the time, I was excited to share his secrets, thrilled to be included, to be treated like an adult, but now I kind of wish maybe I could have stayed a kid a little longer.

He confided things to me and I always thought it was so great, such a big deal, but I don't think that anymore. Now those stupid secrets just make me mad. He left me with all these secrets that I can't share with anyone else and then he just gave up. I'm stuck here with his stupid secrets and he's gone now.

Of course, it's not like I have anyone to tell my secrets to, anyway. Everyone I grew up with and most of the other kids my age have been chosen for an apprenticeship by now. I don't know why I haven't. I've made the rotations we're all supposed to do, but no one asked me to come back, no one wants me to do an apprenticeship and I'm running out of possibilities.

"Come on, Eve. Get a move on."

I nodded, but didn't say anything to my brother as I concentrated on rubbing the leftover sleep from my eyes.

I heard the sound of my brother's boots before he spoke again. "We are so late."

"Yeah. Yeah." I looked up as he walked past. "Why are you in such a hurry today?"

He said something as he moved down the hall, away from me, but my foggy head and the metal plating of the walls muffled his words.

Fortunately, even my late night reading had not kept me from setting out my boots and inner wear before crawling into bed. I was able to quickly dress for the day, even though I was still half asleep.

Only Orin was in the tiny dining area when I walked in. Mom had come in late, so she was most likely still sacked out. Grandmother must have already eaten and reported to her post. Grandad had either spent his night reading. . . he was the only person I knew who had managed to hold onto a few books he had brought with him. . . or he was already out and about somewhere in the complex.

"So, did you find out which apprenticeship you were chosen for, Eve?"

"You know I wasn't, Orin."

"Actually, I didn't know. What are you going to do? You're seventeen. You can't just keep bouncing from one place to another forever."

I tried to keep the venom out of my voice when I spoke, "I am very well aware of that. Thank you."

How could he not understand how frustrating this all was for me? Does he honestly think I enjoy having no place to fit in?

Would he enjoy it?

"I noticed that the hunting parties are looking for some new volunteers, Eve. Have you considered that?"

Grandad's voice sounded behind me just as Grandmother walked into the dining area.

"I don't think that's a very good idea, dear."

"Nonsense. Eve would be a natural."

"I'm not certain Mom would approve." This came from Orin, and it was all I could do to not punch him.

"Weren't you just saying that I can't continue to flit from

section to section forever? I'm supposed to choose an area where I can be useful. . . a place where I can contribute."

"Yes, but. . ."

"But you don't think I can handle it." I fired back quickly, before he could complete his argument.

"That is not what I said and it is not what I meant at all." His face was beginning to turn an alarming shade of red.

"What did you mean, then?" I countered.

"I believe what he meant is that you should not take such chances with your life. This family has already lost more than enough." My grandmother spoke again. . . quietly, her voice filled with a deep sadness I had not heard in months. . . maybe even years.

"But I have to do something to contribute. Why not join the hunting parties? At least I would get to go outside."

Mom's gasp was especially loud in the suddenly quiet room.

I looked up at Grandad, but he only shrugged. Grandmother had busied herself at the cooktop and Orin was looking intently down at his plate as he focused on his food, shoveling it into his mouth faster than I had seen him eat since his last growth jump.

She stood there, staring at me for what felt like an eternity. I sat there, watching her and trying to come up with something to say, but no words came.

Finally, she looked away, moving over to the cooking area. She began to help Grandmother, although I thought I saw her swipe a hand under her eyes, but the movement was so quick I couldn't be certain.

No one else spoke. When I looked back over to Grandad, he shook his head just slightly, so I sat there silently. . . waiting. . . certain that an outburst was forthcoming.

None came.

Mom continued to help Grandmother, and together they finished preparing our breakfast. When Mom placed a plate of food in front of me, I picked up my fork and started eating, forcing small bites past the lump in my throat.

When Grandad had mentioned it, I had only thought of how much I would enjoy the opportunity to get out of the compound, to explore the area around our cave prison. I was sure Mom would tell me I was being incredibly selfish if I ever told her that. Obviously her first reaction had been due to the memory of my father—which had only now come to mind.

But what are the odds of something like that happening? I'll be with a big group of people. Dad had gone out with only a few others and they'd all split up to do their specialized research.

The hunting parties always stick to groups of three or more.

I looked up at Mom as she sat down across from me. There was a definite tinge of red around her eyes—like she was forcing herself to hold back the tears.

What did I just do? Guilt ate away at me and the lump in my throat expanded until I couldn't force the food down anymore.

Carefully, I set my fork down beside my plate.

"Why shouldn't she go?" Grandad's voice was quiet, but firm.

"You know very well why not." Grandmother answered him in a quiet hiss.

I looked over at her in surprise and saw that she was not holding back her tears. They were slipping silently down both cheeks as she stood beside the cooktop, leaning against the wall behind Mom.

"No, we should stop this. The final decision is up to Eve."

I looked back at my mother, shocked at her words.

"Mom, do you really mean that?"

"I do, sweetheart. And I don't want you to let anyone stop you if this is what you decide you really want to do."

A second later she added in a quieter voice, "Lord knows we need all the meat we can get here."

Grandmother let out a little hiss, but Mom kept speaking.

"It's the truth. Being stuck indoors is bad enough on

everyone's health. We need the protein. If that is what Eve wants to do, I think we should support her in it."

Grandmother had an odd expression on her face now. I found myself wondering if it had to do with something else entirely; something I might not even know about.

I watched as Grandmother turned back to the cooktop and Mom began eating breakfast. The silence in the room was so thick at this point, the air around me felt almost like the heavy humidity in the greenhouses, making it difficult to breathe.

After several intense moments, Orin slipped silently from his seat, only pausing to give Mom a quick kiss before making his way out of the room. Grandad was the next to go. When he left, he cleared his throat loudly. Grandmother looked at me, then over to Mom, before shrugging her shoulders and following him out.

"I meant what I said, Eve. You do what you have to do. I would rather have you in the hunting parties than. . ." Her words trailed off and I wanted to ask her what else she was going to say, but a chill was working its way up my spine.

Something Dad had told me flitted into my mind as I watched her expression. There was something like terror in her widened eyes.

I examined the memory as best I could. I could remember Dad telling me once about some teens who never found their proper place in the caves. As hard as I examined the foggy conversation in my mind, I couldn't recall what he had said about it, only that his expression had been much like Mom's was at the moment.

That got me thinking about the pressure I had been feeling lately. No one had said anything specifically, but looking back now with fear in mind, I could see where, with every failed internship, Mom had gotten more tense and worried.

Was there something I should know about what it might mean for me if I did not find my place in the caves?

I opened my mouth to ask, but Mom spoke first.

"I just want you to find your place in the caves. It's very important that we all find our place. We each have to pull our weight if we're going to survive."

And something about the tone of her voice and her carefully chosen words answered my unspoken questions.

I would be in danger if I didn't find a way to contribute—a job I could do permanently.

With that in mind, I nodded sharply, moved back from the table and walked over to where she sat, placing my hand gently over hers.

"Don't worry Mom, I'll find my place. I want to do my part."

FIVE

Arizona Caves

Year 45 A.E.

Day 82

Standing in line behind the small group of teens who were signing up to train for the hunting teams, I looked each of them over, sizing them up the way Grandad had taught me.

He had always said it was important to know your peers; to know who you would need to watch out for, who you could possibly count as an ally, and who you wanted on your side no matter what.

I used that pattern now to group together the other young people who were standing both in front of me and behind, waiting their turn to sign up.

With such a large number of sign ups, I wondered if they would end up breaking the sign ups into more than one training group. I didn't know a lot about the way the hunting parties worked, only that they were responsible for bringing in meat for the entire complex.

Once a month, sign-ups were taken. *Really glad today is the day.* The look in Mom's eyes was still haunting me.

I had been thinking about it since I walked out of our section. As I looked around me at the number of teens who stood around me, I couldn't help but wonder if I were in better company than I realized.

I had always thought I was odd, not fitting in anywhere, but looking around at the faces of the others in line, I could see that I'd been mistaken.

Granted some of them might just want to be hunters. But the odds were on my side—that most of them were more like me than I had ever realized before. Like me, they were struggling to find where they fit in.

The line moved forward and I followed, looking at the mostly empty tables in the common area. There were more people seated in the cavernous room than I'd expected when I'd made my way here earlier. A few had even arrived since I had stepped into line.

It had never occurred to me before now that many of the

people ate here so early in the morning. Eating with my family had given me very few opportunities to visit this area this early in the day. Mostly I had eaten and then rushed off to my current internship.

“Are you nervous?”

I looked behind me at the young woman who had spoken. She was short, like me, but nowhere near as skinny. She was the type of girl the boys always watched whenever she walked through the caves. She had curves in all the right places, but very little excess flesh; just enough to lend a softness to her womanly figure.

She held herself well, though her nervousness had her scrunched in on herself more than a little at the moment. Her hands were twisting and untwisting something as she stood, shifting from foot to foot.

I opened my mouth to reassure her and found that the words suddenly felt false, so I closed my mouth and thought about what answer I could give her that would be true. It didn't take long to figure out that it was indeed nerves I'd been feeling, as they rushed through my veins and jumped around in my stomach, so I answered honestly.

“Yes, I am.”

Her heavy eyelashes swept up to reveal eyes widened in fear. “Really? You aren't just saying that?”

"Really. I didn't think I would be, but I am."

She let out a heavy breath before going on, "I am so glad it's not just me. I thought for sure everyone else here would be excited and I would be like a fish out of water. . . again."

Her words triggered a strange sense of relief. Here was one more affirmation that I was not as alone as I had thought.

"So, what specialty are you going on to when you're done here?"

Or not. That was something that had not occurred to me. I was immediately distracted, trying to size up the others again.

"You are going on to another specialty after this?"

"No actually, I haven't been selected for an apprenticeship."

"Oh." She didn't say anything else. She looked down at the floor and her fingers started twisting again.

Thoughts scrambled around in my head as I tried to figure out what else I could. . . or should. . . say to her.

Nothing came to mind as I stood there. After a moment, the line moved forward again and we both moved forward with it.

"Hey, Eve."

That voice was one I would recognize anywhere. I looked up with a ready smile. Malcolm was one of the few teens in our section who didn't treat me differently. He was always friendly. . . to everyone. "Hey."

Do I dare hope he's signing up, too? If he was, that would make the class much more bearable.

"So, you're signing up to be a hunter, too?" Something about the tone of his words made me wonder what he wasn't saying, but the relief was much stronger, so I shoved the worry away and my smile widened, as I answered him.

"Yes. You, too?"

"Oh, yeah. Dad wants me to get more experience outside with the emphasis on self-defense before I go into vet services. Part of the training involves going out, but they don't really teach defense or anything like that."

Something in his tone when he spoke about vet services made me think the specialty had more to do with his father than with what he wanted.

I didn't miss the fact that his voice held lots of excitement when he'd mentioned hunting. Although I wondered at it, I was more concerned with the information that most of these sign-ups were teens who were heading into other apprenticeships afterward.

"Is everyone headed for something else after this class?"

"Oh no, definitely not. At least a third of the sign-ups are hoping for a permanent placement in the hunting parties."

The girl behind me spoke up then, "Isn't that kind of hard to do, though?"

"Oh yeah, they're real picky about who they take." Malcolm was nodding his head as he answered her, but still looking at me with an odd expression.

The intensity in his eyes finally got the better of me and I snapped at him. "What?"

"Oh, I'm just surprised. I wouldn't have thought your mom or your Grandmother would want you signing up to go outside. You know. . . after. . ." He trailed off without finishing his thought, but it wasn't hard to know where his thoughts were going.

"Well, they aren't exactly thrilled with the idea, but. . ." I shrugged, not certain how much to say about my somewhat precarious situation with an apprenticeship.

Obviously, it wasn't common knowledge that a person had to find something or be in danger—of what I still had no idea—so I tried to shrug it off and stay vague.

Everyone I grew up with and most of the other kids my age have been chosen for an apprenticeship by now. I can't figure out why I haven't. I made the rotations we're all supposed to do, but no one asked me to come back. No one wants me to do an apprenticeship and I'm running out of possibilities.

Maybe I need to try harder.

Or maybe I'm just not cut out for the caves. . . Maybe there's nothing I'm meant to do here.

Maybe I'll end up like Dad.

I hope that's not how it works, but how do I know?

There are so many things no one talks about; things we're not supposed to ask questions about. I wonder why those weren't the kind of things Dad told me about. At least it would be helpful to know what happens to the people who don't seem to fit in here.

What worries me more, though, is that I'm the first one that I know of who has never found a place I fit. The closest thing I can think of to it are the people who mysteriously disappear. And that happens a lot, actually.

Someone doesn't do their job well and they get transferred. But what does that mean?

No one ever explains anything around here. . . especially to a kid.

"Well, you gotta do what you gotta do, I guess." He stood there looking at the two of us another few seconds before speaking again.

"Hey, I gotta go. I'll see you in class though, Eve. And. . ." He looked at the girl behind me again with a questioning smile.

"Oh!" She exclaimed before looking all around her, a startled expression claiming her delicate features, before answering much more quietly, "Anna."

"Well, see you in class Anna. Later, Eve." And he rushed off.

"You know him?" Anna's words were so low, I had to ask her to repeat herself. Even the second time she asked, it was difficult to make out what she said, but I got enough of it to figure out what she was asking.

"Yes, I guess. Sort of." I shrugged a bit as I went on. "He lives in my section, so I see him from time to time."

"What did he mean about your mother not being thrilled with you going outside?" This question was asked in a loud, almost theatrical whisper—and though I had no trouble understanding, I was hesitant to answer. The poor girl was nervous enough.

The line moved and I stepped forward with it. When I stopped again, I turned to look behind me and met her concerned stare. I knew I would not be able to hide the truth from her.

"My father died outside. He was out with a small group and he didn't make it back in time. The gates closed before he could get to them."

Anna's hands flew up to cover the gasp that escaped before she could stop it. It was several long seconds before she recovered enough to speak again.

"I. . . am. . . so. . . sorry." Her head shook back and forth with each word and there was a little gap between the words as well, as if she wanted to put as much emphasis on each one as she could. “That must have been awful.”

There was nothing to say really, so I just stood there. A second later she spoke again.

“You must be very brave. So much more than me.”

Her words took me by surprise. That thought had not even occurred to me. I certainly didn't feel brave. “Oh, I don't know about that.”

“But you are. I didn't even realize how brave until I heard that you chose this all on your own. I would never do this if I didn't have to.”

The line moved again, and I realized it was my turn to sign in. I stepped up to the table and filled in my information as quickly as possible.

Before I finished, I felt someone brush against me from behind and when I looked up, I saw Anna move to one of the sections beside me. Filling in the rest of the form, I tried to decide if I wanted to try and talk to Anna or if I wanted to try and slip away before she could ask any more uncomfortable questions.

The decision was taken out of my hands when I stepped away from the table and saw that she was gone.

Oh well. It's not like I'll ever see her again. What are the odds of us being in the same class. . . especially with how many have signed up for this rotation?

SIX

Arizona Caves

Year 45 A.E.

Day 83

Halfway through my first class, I found myself torn between being glad I'd had the opportunity to spend so much time with grandad, learning things none of the other students possibly could have. . . and worried that my advantage would end up being the death of me.

Grandad had been training me in basic self-defense and as many of the basics of hunting as possible from inside the compound since I could walk, so I already had more than a bit of a jump on the others in my class.

However, I was smart enough to know that, while it could be

good for me in the end, it would also be a very bad idea to show everyone else up—so I pretended to do badly at first.

Of course, there's only so much I can pretend. . .

I could not have prepared for how difficult it was to do something that felt natural for me. . . badly.

Fortunately, fighting was one thing that was relatively easy to fake. Most of the others had at least a hundred pounds on me and, because I was so small, it was easy to avoid the worst of their blows while still making it look like they were doing well. And. . . all the time, I was learning important things about their fighting styles; strengths and weaknesses, habits and tells.

Grandad always said it was important to know your enemy first. Then you couldn't be easily surprised. Also, once you knew what to expect from someone, they were much simpler to defeat.

Since that was the ultimate goal in any fight, I did what I could to learn everything about each of their fighting styles. That way, when it finally came time to show them up, I wouldn't have to worry too much about being their punching bag.

With the other things we were learning, it was harder to do badly. I was skilled enough to miss on purpose with archery and spear hunting, but knife throwing was more difficult. No matter how hard I tried to miss, my reflexes kicked in at the last second and sent the knife right to the target's center every time.

Rifle practice was the one thing that was new to me. I didn't have to pretend to do badly. That might have been the only thing that saved me from being a target for the others.

I had enough skill with aim to know that I could do it well if I wanted to, but the weight of the weapon and the recoil was enough of a struggle to spoil a perfect shot.

Fortunately Adam, the largest boy in the class, was a natural with the rifles. Our instructor made the comment that everyone had something they were a natural at, putting the others at ease.

I breathed a deep sigh of relief at his words. It followed closely enough on the heels of our knife-throwing lesson that anyone who had thought my doing so well was a way of making them look bad, could now chalk it up to my being a natural, without feeling slighted.

“Adam, have you had any previous experience with shooting?”

Adam was shaking his head before the instructor even finished speaking. “No, sir.”

"Well, then, I believe you must be a natural." He turned back to the rest of us before going on.

"As we go through the next few weeks of training, you may all come across a certain area where you have a natural ability."

I thought he might have looked at me a bit too closely, but only for a moment. I breathed a little easier when he looked over at the next student.

"Of course, some of you may well discover that your natural abilities lie elsewhere." He was looking at one of the students across the room. I wondered who he could be speaking of, but I tried not to wonder too much.

That person might not want attention drawn to their inability to compete with the rest of our classmates—just as I didn't want attention drawn to my natural skill.

Of course, as classes went on and we moved to more and more difficult things, it was easier to let some of my own skill show. The best students in class were getting better every day. It felt silly to hold myself back when some of them started to surpass the skill level I had been purposely holding steady at.

I finally admitted to myself that it would be more noticeable if I did not start to improve along with the others.

And then there were the little competitions we held among ourselves. We ran laps daily around the indoor track and worked out for an hour every day before getting started on classes.

Even with running, I had held back in the beginning, because I knew I was much faster than most of the others, but now I was actually letting go some of the time and giving them a real competition.

Coming in first occasionally can't really be considered showing anyone up, because we all win some of them.

The workouts were tougher now, though, and I was still at a tremendous disadvantage, because I was smaller than anyone else in the class. And, while I had good muscle mass, I couldn't hope to out-lift or out-work anyone else. So I had to pick the areas I knew I could present a challenge and really work on those.

As we trained, I thought about the other students and their areas of expertise. I could see that some of them were easily cut out to be guards; Adam was one of those. He had the build of a tank and he hadn't shown an ounce of fear yet.

Some were obviously meant to be hunters, like Malcolm. He had a seemingly limitless amount of patience and he was smart.

He was also a natural at building and setting traps.

Some of the students were clearly not cut out to be either, like Jake and Anna. I couldn't begin to figure out why they had even signed up for the class. I remembered Anna saying something about hoping it would give her an advantage when she started her apprenticeship, but she had absolutely no skill in the area of hunting.

Maybe Jake was doing the same. . . hoping to put his limited skills to use with another area of expertise.

Both of them must be something that required them to go outside the gates, but not be especially adept at fighting or hunting. . . just enough to protect themselves and those around them if it was necessary.

I still couldn't figure out where I fit, though. I had hoped to find my place with these classes, but once I had done my training and then my rotation with the hunting parties, I would be right back where I'd started.

Maybe I'm holding back too much. It might be that I needed to really show my skill in order to get noticed.

Besides, I told myself, *we're far enough into the training and enough of the other students have improved so that I won't really be showing anyone else up if I start doing my very best.*

So I started to let my true skill show in a few areas.

And when there was no resistance from the other students, I

let more and more of it show, until I was using my full skill in every area.

It was surprising to realize that the other students were actually giving me a good run in each skill set. Not the same ones in every area, but at least one presented a true competition in each area.

It was good to feel the thrill of competition, to really use my skill, to realize that I was helping to hone the others' skills—and fortunately, no one seemed to notice that while each one of us had an exceptional skill in at least one area, I was matching them or excelling in every area.

SEVEN

Arizona Caves

Year 45 A.E.

Day 98

The metallic thump of a tray caught my attention and I jerked my head up to find the source of the racket.

"Hey, Eve." Sierra nodded as she slid onto the narrow bench opposite me. "Whatcha workin on?"

She reached across the table, but I pulled the worn paper out of reach before she could snatch it away, carefully folding it and sliding it into my jacket's inner pocket.

"That doesn't look like something for class."

"It's not." I struggled to smooth the irritation from my voice. It wasn't her fault she didn't know what this scrap of paper meant to me. . . or that I'd been carrying it around for nearly five years now and was still desperately afraid to let anyone know I had it.

"O. . . K. . . then."

Before she said anything else, the clang of a metal tray against the metal table announced the arrival of someone else, and Lily dropped into the seat next to Sierra.

"Who else has had enough of this waiting?"

"Oh, come on. It's only been like a week extra." This came from behind me, but before I could turn to see who had spoken, Malcolm was sliding onto the seat next to me.

"Hey, Eve. How's your mom?"

"Hi, Malcolm. She's good. Tense. . . you know." I tried shrugging it off, but the feeling that he could see right through it was the least of my worries.

Things in the caves still hadn't settled down.

In the almost three weeks since the 2 A.M. alarm, people had come to be more on edge than I'd ever seen them. Everyone was looking at everyone else like they were guilty; like they were hiding something, or hiding someone.

But in the last three weeks, no other criminals had been

punished and the leader had not been discovered, so the tension in the caves had been almost as thick as the snow storms that had prevented hunting parties from going out.

The storms lately had gotten so bad, even the gates haven't been able to hold them back. As a result, everyone had been stuck inside the complex and people were starting to get a little stir crazy.

Everyone was pretty much used to being stuck in the compound.

That's normal.

No one went outside the gates unless they had permission, protective gear and special training, but being confined to the caves, stuck indoors for almost two weeks with a criminal—a possible rebel leader living among them—was making everyone a little nuts.

"Oh, come on. For weeks, we've gone over the same stuff. If we don't know it by now, we don't know it."

The harshness in Jake's voice pulled my attention to the conversation that had continued around me.

"Hey, I for one am not a bit sorry that going outside has to wait until the storms clear." Adam's voice surprised me. He was the one I would have pegged as the most impatient to get outside and hunt something.

Obviously, Jake was just as surprised, because he sat there for the longest time with a goofy expression on his face.

"So, what did you think of that trap class?" Malcolm's voice was quiet, obviously meant just for me, so I turned to him.

"It was interesting."

His laugh took me by surprise.

"What?"

"I'm glad to see that we've finally found something you're not better at than everyone else in the whole compund."

I struggled to control my reaction. How had he caught on to that? *I've been so careful. . .* or I thought I had anyway.

"You know exactly what I mean. You've been holding back from the beginning. Don't try to deny it. I've spent too many years watching you to doubt it."

"You've been. . ."

"That's right. We live in the same section. I have to walk behind your family every time there's a drill. We had the same first classes."

His words made it sound like it was simply a part of life—a coincidence—that he had been watching because of proximity or convenience, but there was something about the tone. . . and the fact that he looked down and stared very intently at his plate after he said it.

"Hey, Eve, did you hear?" Anna slid onto the bench on the other side of me. I could hear that same tremor in her voice that had been so obvious the day we'd first met. "They're saying the storms could clear up as early as tomorrow."

"Really, tomorrow? Don't toy with me, Anna." This came from Jake, the first thing he'd said since Adam had spoken up a few minutes earlier.

"Quit it, Jake. Anna might not realize you're teasing." Lily added a smack to Jake's upper arm, and it didn't look like a love pat to me. Everyone in class knew all about their relationship, so Lily must have thought Jake was tougher than he looked.

I looked over at Anna. It was no surprise to see the deep crimson blush that started at her cheeks and disappeared beneath her collar.

"You quit it, Lil. Sheesh. Anna knows I'm just a big joker."

While Jake and Lily argued, I picked at the food on my plate and thought about Anna.

I had watched the other students in our class getting better—and was relieved when I actually had to work to keep up with some of them. It felt good to actually use my skills, kind of like sharpening a blade.

But Anna. . . she was not improving at all.

Though she had a talent for building intricate traps, she had failed miserably with setting them up. She had also excelled at all of the weapon building we'd learned, but when it came to shooting any of them, she was hopeless.

Clearly she was adept at the technical work, which would serve her well when she transferred to the communications area. She would likely be instrumental in the preservation of equipment we could not replace and could not survive without.

But she would make a terrible hunter.

"How did you hear about the storms, Anna?" Malcolm spoke up from my other side, drawing me out of my thoughts.

"Oh, my mother is in meteorology. She told me this morning."

"Wow. That's handy."

Anna must have blushed again, because Malcolm smiled, but said nothing else—and I could almost feel the heat coming off her face beside me.

I looked up just as Jude slipped onto the bench across from me, right next to Jake and Lily. He didn't say a word to anyone, just applied himself to his meal, looking around at the people seated nearby with what looked like a half-smile.

When his eyes met mine, I thought his smile might have twitched a bit, but his gaze did not stay connected to mine. He looked on around, settling for a moment on Anna and moving on again.

He finally looked back down at his own plate, and though I watched him, he did not look up again until we were all standing to leave.

Adam started the exodus. He stood and said something under his breath, stepping away from the table with his empty tray.

Jake and Lily waited only a moment or two before slipping away quietly behind him. Anna muttered something beside me before she, too, slid off the bench and disappeared.

When I looked over, I saw that Malcolm was getting up.

"Later, Eve."

I nodded and then turned back to see that Jude and I were the only two left at the table. I debated with myself about whether or not I should try to strike up a conversation.

Though neither of us is exactly known for conversation. I nearly laughed at the thought. I was pretty sure I'd not heard a single word from Jude the entire three weeks we'd been in class.

When I looked up again though, he was gone, leaving just silently as he'd come. Searching the cavernous great room did me no good. Our group had arrived early, when the room had been sparsely populated. Now, the room was filled near to bursting with bodies.

EIGHT

Arizona Caves

Year 45 A.E.

Day 101

It was three weeks after the public execution before the storms finally subsided enough to venture past the compound gates.

The next afternoon, our class was introduced to an area in the complex that none of us had known existed.

Our instructor stepped up to the door of a room none of us had entered before. Before he raised a hand to knock, it opened and he ushered us inside. We were all a little surprised to discover a tiny woman standing in front of rows of weapons and other related gear filling the immense room.

She stood there with a very grim expression. She held her arms crossed tightly over her chest, feet planted firmly, legs slightly spread.

She might be tiny, but she looked formidable.

As we filed in, we spread out in a line facing her. Our instructor stepped up, moving to the front. He looked us over carefully, before speaking.

"This is our master-at-arms. She is in charge of all weapons and outdoor gear." He paced back and forth in front of us as he spoke. The woman's eyes followed his every move, but she didn't say a single word.

"You are to see her any time you are assigned to be outdoors. Your outdoor gear and weapons will be assigned to each of you personally, but you must return everything each time you come back inside." He paused, waiting to see if there were any questions, but no one said a word. He turned to the woman, who nodded to him, then turned and walked toward the towering shelves located directly behind her.

Our instructor followed, motioning for us to follow his lead. The master-at-arms stopped about halfway down the aisle. Picking up a crossbow and a quiver of metal-tipped arrows, she pulled a small object out of her pocket and clicked a button on the side of it. A bright screen appeared.

Several gasps of surprise were heard throughout the room.

Most of us had never seen a computer, let alone a hand-held

one. She pointed the top of the device toward a section of the crossbow and a moment later, it made a beeping sound. Then she turned and handed the crossbow to Jude, the tallest boy in our class. He was not first in line, but she obviously had a method and no one thought to question her, especially since we were still distracted by the tiny computer in her hand.

She turned and walked several more feet, glancing at items hanging on the wall and sitting on the shelves, before stopping again. She looked over at us, stopping when her eyes met mine.

She pulled a wooden bow off the wall and a long quiver of arrows from below it. I watched as she repeated the process she'd done before with the hand-held computer.

The bow had to be the most beautiful thing I had ever seen. The wood was a rich, chocolate brown, with intricately hand-carved etchings along the length of it. The arrows were equally beautiful. I could only see the feathers sticking out of the end of the quiver, but they were sleek and smooth as silk.

Could they be for me? Had she been looking at me before she picked it up? Could I be so lucky?

And then she turned and handed them to me. Since everyone around me was watching her intently, I felt safe running my hand up and down the smooth length of the bow as we all moved forward. I was so intent on the bow in my hands, I jumped when she held out a sheaf of knives to me. I breathed a sigh of relief as she reached up for additional knives to scan and then pass to others around me.

A minute later, she handed me another knife. This one was longer than the others. I carefully put the quiver of arrows and the bow over my shoulder. Then I took a moment to look at the sheaf of knives and compared them to the single knife.

The sheaf was one that rolled out and it looked like it would attach to an arm or leg. There were little strings that I could see on each edge. They were neatly tucked into the part that was rolled up. I could only see two of the knives, but they looked very dangerous—short, sharp and very smooth. These would fly far and fast.

Silent. Deadly. They'll be great for hunting.

The minutes seemed to stretch into hours as we followed this tiny woman from aisle to aisle as she searched out weapons and assigned them out. Finally it looked as if she was done. Then she picked up a rifle, logged it into the hand-held computer and passed it on to our instructor. He was the only one assigned a rifle.

We reached the end of the row, turned the corner, and walked into another room identical to the one we'd left, except this one was filled with racks of clothing and other gear. The master-at-arms went through the same process in this room. She handed out clothing, boots, thick coats with fur-lined hoods, and packs of different sizes and designs.

When it was my turn, she handed a medium-sized pack to me. I realized it wasn't empty, but something told me this was not the time to go through it, although curiosity was burning within me.

When she had outfitted the entire group with what we would need to survive outdoors, I suddenly realized no words had been spoken—not by anyone—and we had made a complete circle back to where we had begun. Soon we found ourselves following our instructor out the hatch. He stopped at another room two doors over and again motioned for us to follow.

I glanced back over my shoulder as I moved through the doorway, and the tiny woman was standing in the same place she'd been when we arrived.

When I moved into the room, the first thing I noticed was that there were lockers on the wall facing us. Each one had a name and a number on the front. When I looked closer, I realized it was a citizen ID number. I looked to the right of me and the wall of lockers stretched as far as I could see; the far wall appeared as a tiny square at the end of a slowly shrinking line of narrow metal doors.

Our instructor moved toward the wall at the right side of the room and gestured toward the lockers in front of us. Everyone began searching for the locker with their own name. It didn't take long for me to find my locker. The lock was a print and scan, which surprised me.

What is so important? Why would we need such heavy security?

I pressed my thumb against the small round pad and a panel opened in front of me at eye level, prompting me to lean forward and allow the laser to scan my retina. Immediately, the lock clicked and the metal hatch swung open. All along the wall on either side of me, the same thing was happening, followed by oohs and other sounds of enthusiasm from both directions.

I really can't blame them. It was no surprise that they were making such a fuss over it.

This type of security was so rare, I had only ever seen it once; in the hallway to the chancellor's offices. Dad had taken me through one time. There had been print pads at every door and scanners at most of them, too.

"If you'll look into your lockers, you'll see that there are places to hang up your weapons and store your knives. This is very important. All your weapons are to be left here in your individual lockers before we leave here today."

Like everyone else, I had looked over at him when he began speaking. I noticed that he looked around at the class with a hard look before going on.

"You will have noticed that security is top-notch. You. . . and only you are able to open this side. The master-of-arms is the only person who can open the other side. Every time we come in, she will be checking and cleaning your weapons. Once that is done, they will be stored in your lockers, but there will be a message on the locker to tell you when she is working. Another will appear when she is finished and has replaced the weapons."

All around me heads were nodding. At least one person had swung their locker door around so they could look for the area where the message would display. I wanted to do the same, but I didn't want to simply follow the crowd so I waited, listening as the instructor continued.

"You will have access to your locker only as long as you are assigned to the hunting detail. If you move on, you will no longer have access to your locker." Something about the way he said it—and the strange, cold, hard expression reflected in his eyes when he looked at me—sent a shiver racing down my spine.

He quickly looked away, but the icy chill remained. I half-listened to everything else he said, as my thoughts raced. Was it possible he had somehow figured out that I had secrets?

He seemed to know that I was hiding my natural abilities in class.

But what would he do about it?

And what could he have guessed that I know?

The chill stayed with me as we put away our weapons. He didn't look my way as he moved past me and into the hall to wait for the rest of the class to finish up.

As we walked back to the classroom, he continued to speak about pertinent details. He told us that the packs, along with the long, plain knives, were the only things we were allowed to keep with us—and that we would need to keep the packs in our lockers or in the classroom with us at all times.

He also mentioned that we would need to turn our basic compasses in to each unit's section leaders so they could be reassigned.

We were halfway back to our classroom before someone got up the nerve to ask the instructor the question that had been burning in all of our minds. . . well, except maybe my own.

I was surprised though, to hear Alan's voice, the smallest boy in the class. He was not the youngest among us, but he was apparently a late bloomer.

"Why doesn't she talk?"

I was also surprised at how calm he sounded when he asked. His voice didn't squeak at all when he spoke—and it had been squeaking for weeks.

The instructor paused a moment before answering. "To be honest, I don't know. I've asked others, but no one seems to know. We just know that she doesn't speak—ever."

The next question came from Anna. "Do other people talk to her? I mean, how does she know what someone wants?"

The instructor let out a short bark of a laugh before answering.

"I've tried talking to her before. There were times I was told to requisition something specific or when I was doing something different and I thought I needed something special, but I never had to tell her anything. She always went right to what I needed like she'd known it all along."

Now I was curious and I couldn't seem to stop the words from popping out, even though I really should know better by now than to ask questions without weighing every word. "And she never responded, ever?"

His answer was immediate. "No. I don't know anyone who's ever heard her talk. As far as I can tell, she's not partnered with anyone. And everyone says she sleeps in the requisition room." He shrugged, but kept talking.

"I don't know about that. It's just what I've heard. I do know it's a waste of breath to talk to her. And I know she does her job very well. She always makes certain you have everything you need when you're going out."

By this time we had reached our classroom. The instructor looked around, waiting until he had everyone's attention. "The next part will be the toughest. You need to familiarize yourselves with all the gear—most of it is probably unfamiliar to you—before you'll be allowed to venture outside. You must know how to use everything the master-at-arms has given you before you go through those gates. By now you should already know how to use the weapons, so concentrate on the other items in your pack."

We spent almost an hour going through the packs the master-of-arms had given us. Most of the students upended their packs and then sorted through the pile in front of them. I took a more measured approach, emptying the pack slowly, lining things up as I pulled them out and then examining each item carefully before packing it away again just where it had been initially found.

There were several lengths of rope—each one a different thickness and meticulously coiled—plus a mesh bag full of carabiner clips in a variety of sizes and types. Knowing it would make it easier to grab the one I would need quickly, I took time to empty the bag and then clip the different types together.

Next, I sorted through a well-stocked, emergency first-aid kit. It included the standard bandages and antiseptic sprays, but it also held medicines I'd never seen before and several types of bandages that looked as if they were meant for major injuries.

I held the first-aid kit in my hand for several long seconds, just staring at it, before packing it away again. This was the one thing I knew I would make every effort to keep from Mother and Grandmother. While Grandad would applaud that we were well prepared, Mother and Grandmother would likely see the first-aid supplies only as a painful reminder of the danger that faced each of us each time we set foot outside the complex.

The remainder of the contents jumbled a bit in my head even while I took out each piece and examined it carefully, having lost any appeal in the sudden overwhelming certainty that—somehow—this was a very bad idea.

Fortunately, we'd all had to learn how to read a compass in early education. We were actually required to carry a basic compass with us wherever we went because the caves were extensive and it was sometimes too easy to get lost.

However, we'd been through a refresher course early on in this class and had already been through the extended functions that were attached to the compasses in our packs. These were much more complex than the basic ones everyone received when they were kids.

It took the rest of the time to go over how everything else worked and a few students stayed over to ask more questions. But we managed to feel almost prepared for our journey outside.

That evening I mentioned to Mom that we would be going outside the next day. I waited for her to say something, but she just nodded her head slightly, although I could see the stress of it in her eyes.

Clearly she didn't want me to go outside, but she didn't say it. . . and I couldn't help but wonder why she kept silent. Part of me wanted her to speak up, to argue with me, to demand that I stay.

But she did none of those things.

My grandparents were on early shifts for the week and they both happened to be home for dinner so we all ate together. Orin had also come for dinner, though he didn't talk to anyone during the whole meal.

He'd never been much of a talker, not since what happened with dad anyway, but he had been especially quiet for the last three weeks. I hadn't really given it a lot of thought, but sitting here tonight, with going outside so much on my mind, something occurred to me that had not before.

Was it possible, just maybe, that one of those kids had been a friend of his? There were only two years between us, but we didn't share any of the same interests. He'd been chosen for a tech internship when he was only seven so he was almost always busy with that.

Most nights he wasn't even here to eat with us.

And that was another odd thing. Now that I thought about it, he'd been here for dinner every night for the last three weeks. I wanted desperately to ask him what was going on, but I didn't want to add to Mom's worry by bringing up something that could start a fight.

Obviously, he had a reason for being here—and for being extra quiet. Maybe I could find time to ask him about it after my outdoor lesson tomorrow.

And maybe when Mom isn't around, so she won't have to worry about both of us.

I noticed Mom watching me, but as soon as I looked up and met her searching gaze, she looked down at my plate. I hoped she was only wondering why I wasn't eating.

Not wanting her to draw any conclusions about it, I made a show of chewing, working on the piece of bread that was still in my mouth from the roll I'd bitten into a few minutes ago.

She was still looking at my plate though, so she likely didn't notice.

I tried to chew faster and was reaching for my fork when she finally looked over at my Grandfather. I couldn't see the expression on her face clearly, but he nodded at her and then smiled reassuringly so I figured her expression was probably one of panic.

"So Eve, I just bet your class is feeling pretty confident about tomorrow. They've had some extra time to get ready, what with the storms. Handy, that is, huh?"

I knew his words were supposed to be encouraging, but they didn't strike me that way.

I hadn't even realized with all of the other things I had been worrying over the last three weeks, but there was a tightness in my chest when he mentioned going outside.

I opened my mouth, but nothing—absolutely nothing—came out. So I shut it again before anyone noticed and nodded my head, putting a big smile on my face at the same time.

He was looking right at me, so he definitely noticed, but I was hoping no one else had. Mom was still looking at Grandad, and Grandmother had her head bowed, so she was probably praying and not paying any attention to us.

When I thought about it, I realized she'd been doing a lot of praying lately, but she never talked about it, so I wasn't really sure if it was because of me or if it was for the young children who had been sent out into the cold three weeks ago.

She might have been an important person back when the caves were built, but her importance had quickly diminished after the government official she had been aide to, had not made it to the caves in time.

She talked about that time less and less now, but I remembered her saying that she had been useful. . . for a time, anyway.

As a little kid I hadn't noticed anything weird about what she had said or the way she'd said it. But now—knowing what I did—I could look at it from an entirely new perspective.

I remembered her telling us that a lot of people had looked to her for advice and help with organizing people and shipments as they had come into the caves. Being an aide to a high government official was something that had given her a lot of experience with organizing schedules and assignments for a large office—so she had been well-suited to the job.

However, once everything had begun to calm down, the system that we had now had been established—at least until something more permanent could be put back into place. And since she'd been expecting my mother at the time, she had been relegated to something that was considered to be less of a strain on her condition; minding the little kids.

She had been given the option later to change jobs, but she must have truly enjoyed wrangling little kids because she'd decided to stick with it.

Which probably means she knew every one of the kids who had been in that group.

That was a perfect reason to pray; although it wasn't exactly something she would talk about to anyone outside of our little family.

Praying was not a very popular thing to do in the caves. It wasn't exactly outlawed, but it also was not encouraged. I had never actually heard anyone outside of the family talk about praying. . . much less about God.

In fact, Grandmother was the only one in the family I had ever seen pray out in the open like this. If Mom did pray, she must do it in the privacy of her own room. But Grandmother had never hidden her faith.

I wasn't sure if I bought into the idea of someone. . . some invisible guy in the sky who moved us all around like chess pieces to suit himself.

And that made me wonder about why she was really praying. I'd heard it often enough – that you had to believe in God to get to Heaven.

Could she be praying for me? Could she be worried about me? Is she thinking I'm going to die out there. . . like dad?

It only took a moment for me to be certain that was it. She was worried for me. . . *just like everyone else.*

Because of what happened to my father, because of what happened three weeks ago. . .

Likely even because I was so small and everyone was certain I couldn't handle the rigors of hunting?

And just why is everyone so sure I can't handle those things?

Suddenly I was angry, I wanted to scream at someone, anyone. I wanted to hit something. Why was everybody so sure I was totally and completely inept!

I can do things. I'm capable of doing a lot of things!

And that was just things I'd been taught to do. It wasn't even taking into consideration the things no one even knew about, like keeping important secrets or beating the crap out of someone twice my size.

I opened my mouth, prepared to yell and scream at everyone around the table, but when I looked up, I looked right into my mother's eyes. The look on her face told me everything I needed to know.

She knew exactly what I was thinking. And she probably knew why. She was my mother. She knew me better than anyone.

Well, except for the secrets my father had asked me to keep from her.

When my father had discovered secrets he wanted to share with someone, had he told my mother? No, he'd shared them with me.

He had cautioned me to keep them between the two of us because it wasn't safe to tell anyone else, even my own mother. At the time I had been too young to question him, but now, especially after what had happened two weeks ago, I was beginning to look at the whole thing differently.

Why couldn't I trust my own mother? Why hadn't he trusted her? What was so serious about the little things he had shared with me that it wasn't safe to tell anyone else? And why hadn't I questioned it until now?

What about the recent public execution that had spurred me to examine it in such a way? After seventeen years, I really should be used to the harsh punishments, and the way everyone took it in stride.

I should be used to it, but for some reason, I obviously was not.

It was then that I realized it was not the execution that was haunting me. It was the children themselves, the small boy with no shoes and the boy about my age looking so defiant.

It was the fact that a group of children had been sentenced to death and no adults had joined them. No adult had stood up for them. No adults had stepped forward and taken the punishment for them. . . or with them.

NINE

Arizona Caves

Year 45 A.E.

Day 102

The following day—two days after the storms let up—we had our first outdoor class. We spent a lot more time getting ready than I expected, but finally it was time for us to go out.

We walked toward the large gates, wearing more survival gear than I would have thought possible, laden down with packs and weapons—and nerves.

I followed the rest of the class toward the enormous gates that protected us from danger. I held my breath as they opened slowly.

Our instructor had mentioned that we were going to get an early start, but I had not put that together with having to actually witness the gates opening before we went out.

As the doors moved apart, I felt an odd sensation in my stomach and a tightening in my chest.

I couldn't have breathed if I wanted to—though I did try.

The thought of my last time standing near these gates was suddenly prominent in my mind. Grisly visions of walking through piles of frozen corpses danced into my head, sending a wave of nausea through me.

I didn't want to admit that my mom or grandparents could have been right to worry, but I knew then. . . that they had been.

I wasn't ready for this.

The tremendous noise of metal against metal brought another memory to mind; watching my father from the top of the walls. Once it popped into my head, it started going round and round, adding to the sick feeling that was threatening to bring with it a cold sweat.

I struggled against my own thoughts, trying desperately to focus on our training and on all of the things my Grandfather had taught me over the years.

If I had any hope of surviving out there, I had to focus. And I knew it. I had to stop thinking about such dangerous things or they might just get me killed.

Fortunately, at that moment, the class began to move through the doors. I looked up at the tops of the gates and the walls on either side. They were so high, the people on the top looked tiny to me and I was certain I would look tiny to them, too.

My Grandad was up there somewhere.

Is he watching me? Is he even on this side, where he can see the gates? I knew he was on duty, but I also knew the guards were moved around frequently. They had a very complex schedule that I had never understood.

It was something to do with keeping fresh eyes on each area and keeping the guards themselves from getting too bored.

Another memory popped into my head when I thought about that schedule. My father had told me there was more to it than that. He'd been explaining how important it was to check with the officer on duty before I headed up to take Grandad dinner because they moved him around a lot and I wouldn't want to get lost up there.

"There's something about the way they move the guards around that just doesn't sit right with me. I don't know what it is yet. But I have a feeling there might be more to it than most of the people here realize."

I gasped as the echo of his words receded in my head. I hadn't thought of that. . . maybe ever. . . since he had told me, so many years ago. At the time, his words hadn't made a great deal of sense to me.

Now they made almost a sickening kind of sense.

Did my father stumble onto something he shouldn't have? Something he shouldn't know? Something dangerous?

What if he hadn't been late coming back to the complex that day? What if it had not been an accident—what had happened to him that day?

Was my father murdered?

The idea shocked me.

Where had that even come from?

I had been right there, looking at him. He had been all alone as he struggled to reach the gate in time. How could it have been anything other than a tragic accident? The very idea was ridiculous.

It was a crazy idea to even think and I knew it.

But the thought was there in my head and somehow, in this moment, it didn't seem so ridiculous or crazy.

It made me think about that early morning a few weeks ago. Had there been more to that than anyone else had known—certainly no one who had been dragged from their bed at two in the morning.

No one really knew what had happened, anyway. I had discreetly asked around and no one had been able to tell me any more than I already knew.

Could there have been something sinister to it, something other than what we were led to believe? Is that even possible?

Was this why my father had made a point of telling me to keep these things to myself? Separately, they seemed silly, unimportant, tiny, and nonsensical even. . . but together they seemed the thoughts of a conspiracy. Together they appeared to be the makings of a plot that could go so deep that it had enough weight behind it to get someone killed, maybe even more than one someone.

Which brought me right back to my father.

What if his death was not an accident?

What if someone purposely delayed him or somehow got him hopelessly lost. . . or even stranded him somewhere on purpose?

Could he have been murdered? Was it really so impossible?

And if he was murdered, who was responsible? And why?

Why would anyone have wanted to kill my father?

Our little group had been moving further from the gates as all of this was revolving around in my head. We were almost to the trees, the same trees where I had last seen my father.

Those trees had figured into more than one of my nightmares over the years.

And now, standing just in front of them, I could see that those fears were not as silly as I had always thought. The trees were creepy. They were frightening. And we were heading right toward them.

Unfortunately, they didn't get any less scary as we got closer to them. If it was possible, they might actually be even creepier. They were much taller up close and that was saying something, considering the height of the walls around the complex.

The one thing that surprised me was my reaction to the trees. Scary they might be, creepy and very tall, but they did not frighten me. . . not really.

I felt no tightening in my chest, no difficulty breathing, none of the things I had felt just a few moments ago.

I did, however, think back to the memory of that terrible day again. I could remember watching my father walk out of the towering mass of trees.

I also remembered watching him walk back into them. The last glimpse I'd had of him was of him being swallowed up by the mass of tall, dark trees.

And it made me wonder.

Why did he go back into the trees? It made no sense.

He was so close to the compound.

Why didn't he try harder? Why hadn't he tried to reason with someone at the gate? There was a communication post just outside the gates. He should have been able to do something.

He should not have just given up like he did.

My thoughts forced me to realize just how angry I was with him. After all these years, I was more than angry with him. I was furious. It might not be his fault that he didn't make it. It might not be his fault that the stupid rules were there. But it was his fault that he'd given up. He had given up. He had walked away.

He saw me, I know he did.

And knowing that I was there, watching his every move, screaming out to him, he had chosen to walk away. He had walked away from me. He hadn't even tried, he'd just given up.

It had taken coming out here. . . seeing this place up close. . . to realize just how angry I was at him.

We spent the entire day outside. We went over all of the things we had been learning in class; how to find wood for a fire, how to start a fire with only wood. We climbed trees and followed animal trails.

We even did a little hunting.

At one point, our instructor split us up into three groups. There were two groups of four and my group of three. There were eleven in the class and I had ended up in the smaller group.

I had a moment to wonder if the instructor had something against us or if maybe, just maybe, he had seen that I was more skilled than I was letting on and he knew I would even things up.

Whatever the reasons behind it, I was determined to outshine the other two groups.

We split off and headed in different directions, but as soon as we were far enough away to not be heard, I stopped the others.

"Listen. We're at a slight disadvantage here, so I think we need a plan." I looked at them and they looked back at me. Lily was not a planner; she was a doer. I knew this about her and I knew it also put us at a disadvantage, but I didn't say it. It didn't take long to see that I didn't need to. At the moment she was looking more than a little trapped, almost like she knew we were in trouble.

I could tell Malcolm was thinking the same thing. I could only hope that the two of us might balance her out. At least Malcolm had more pluses than negatives on his side. He was a natural with traps and that would definitely work in our favor, *if we have time for them.*

He was also smart and I really hoped his natural caution might be able to make up for Lily's impetuousness.

Right now they were both looking pretty panicked and I knew I had to put a stop to that before I did anything else or this competition would be over before it had even begun.

“Look. I know what you're both thinking. You're thinking we can't possibly win this thing. You're thinking we might as well just give up now, but we're not going to do that. So just get rid of that idea right now.”

I was surprised to see them nodding. And they both visibly relaxed—and smiled at me, so I nodded in return. Since neither of them stepped forward with any ideas, I plowed on ahead with my own.

“I'm thinking we need to stick together, work as a team. I have a feeling Adam's group is going to split up because they're all going to feel like they have to prove themselves. On the other hand, Jude's team will probably try, but they're pretty much incapable of working as a team, so I think it will work against them in the end."

They were nodding again. I didn't know if they had picked up on it too or if they were just agreeing with me.

"I think it's really important that we work together. We all have strengths and we all have weaknesses. I know we can find a way to beat them if we just stick together."

Lily looked excited at that.

"So, what do we do?"

And I smiled because I knew that was exactly the attitude we needed.

TEN

Arizona Caves

Year 45 A.E.

Day 118

Malcolm and I sat high in the tree, watching his new trap. He had come up with the idea almost a week after our first class expedition and had started building it immediately. Since we went out every week now to train and hunt, he had the perfect chance to test it out.

Lily had learned a lot more about patience in the weeks since that first trip, so she was off hunting alone, while we waited to see if this new trap would be a success.

If it worked the way it was supposed to, it would bring down some pretty big prey. It would take the strength of both of us to drag whatever we caught back to the complex.

While we waited, I watched Malcolm.

He had more patience than anyone I knew. As for me, I was beginning to get bored, just sitting here with nothing to do but wait. Not to mention, it gave me too much free time.

Time to think was something I had been carefully avoiding these last few weeks. Too much thinking made me worry about all of the things that I was angry about. And being angry at my father made me want to tell someone. . . anyone. . . every single secret he had ever shared with me.

Even though the desire was very strong, there was something that stopped me. Something deep within me told me it would be a very, very bad idea to tell anyone about things my father had shared with me. Whether they seemed important to me or not wasn't the point. They had obviously been important enough, since my father had frightened me more than I thought possible. The fact was, it had scared the crap out of me, when he told me that it could get me, him, and the rest of the family killed if I ever told anyone.

Logically, I knew it was possible he had only said that because I was young and prone to chatter a lot. But it was also possible he was completely on the level. I was not prepared to put my whole family in danger because I was mad at him.

So I had been avoiding time alone as much as possible.

Whenever we were not in class, I was working out, or getting in some extra target practice, or volunteering for extra jobs around the complex—anything I could do to keep myself busy.

It also served to help me at night. I was so exhausted by the time I fell into bed, it didn't take any time for me to fall asleep —which kept me from thinking too much.

If the family noticed anything out of the ordinary, they hadn't said anything about it yet. Maybe I was lucky and they chalked it up to me wanting to be the best in my class.

I had mentioned the extra practice a lot and I knew Grandad would have seen my name on the sign-up sheet for the target range often enough. I could only hope they had put those things together and figured that was all I was up to.

Not to mention, I've always been a naturally competitive person, so it should come together and make sense to them.

At least, that's what I told myself.

But here I was, in a tree with absolutely nothing to distract me and I couldn't even talk to take my mind off everything. Talking was a bad idea for a hunter. Any noise at all could scare an animal off and you might never even know it. So I sat there with Malcolm on the branch opposite me and we waited and watched, hoping the new trap would work.

We both turned our heads when we heard loud crashing sounds in the brush coming from our left.

"Either that's a really big animal. . ." Malcolm's words trailed off.

We were both obviously thinking the same thing. We looked at each other and I was sure the panic I saw on his face mirrored my own.

"We didn't exactly consider that possibility."

I knew we had maybe three seconds before someone came crashing into our trap. I also knew I had to think fast. I couldn't think of anything else to do, so I moved as quickly as I could and pulled back the arrow I'd already notched into my bow and let it fly.

Thankfully, it hit the mark and the trap was triggered. The movement was so quick, it was difficult to even see it, even right there in front of us. Not two seconds after it snapped, Adam came barreling through—with a very large animal following closely behind him.

He was screaming and running wildly, knocking tree branches out of his path and flattening bushes.

I heard Malcolm mutter something under his breath. It might have been a forbidden word, but I hadn't heard it clearly enough to know for sure.

I knew how he felt though. Adam would scare away any other game that might come near us for a good long while.

The animal behind him was our only chance, so I notched another arrow and aimed for the head. I didn't recognize the beast, but the head was always a pretty safe bet.

I let the arrow fly.

My breath puffed out in relief when it hit its' target and the beast crashed to the ground inches from Adam.

It was several seconds before Adam realized the beast was down and stopped running. When he did, he dropped to his knees and I could hear him trying to catch his breath. Malcolm and I looked at each other again and I was surprised to hear the same slightly nervous laughter coming from him.

Adam looked up at us and shook his head.

"I'm glad you're amused."

Something about that sent us into another round of laughter. We were so distracted by our own amusement; neither of us noticed when Adam got to his feet.

Malcolm noticed first. I saw the look of panic in his eyes just before his head turned. I followed the direction he was looking —to see Adam standing right at the base of our tree.

I could imagine the panic I saw on Malcolm's face had to do with Adam's size and his tendency to beat up on those of us in class who were smaller than him. . . *which was everyone.*

The smile on Adam's face did not look like one of a bully's. It was more like that of a friend. Then he did something even more unexpected—he began laughing!

Malcolm and I looked at each other again. The panic on Malcolm's face had been replaced by confusion. I was sure it showed on mine, too. We both looked back down when we heard Adam's voice. There was no venom, no embarrassment and no anger in it—only amusement.

"I know one of you took it out, but I think I ought to get a little bit of the credit for leading it right to you." And he was laughing again before he even finished talking.

I looked over at Malcolm, working to inject as much warmth into my voice as I could, while I tried to communicate my thoughts with my eyes and my body language.

"I can go along with that."

We couldn't stay up here forever. Eventually he would get mad and—at the least—make us drag that huge carcass back to camp without his help. Apparently Malcolm understood my subtle message because he nodded. "Sounds fair to me."

I returned his nod and then carefully started picking my way down the tree. After a moment, he followed me down. Once we were both on the ground, he spoke again, voicing what I had just been thinking. His voice was infused with just enough humor.

"We have to share the credit. There's no way we can get this monster back to camp without your help."

I watched in awe of how skilled he was at picking up on what Adam obviously needed. His words were exactly what Adam needed to hear because he doubled over with laughter. When he stood back up, he clapped Malcolm on the back, and even though it almost knocked Malcolm over, we could both see that Adam was not angry, he was just showing his delight at Malcolm's words.

Even with the three of us working together, it took quite a while to figure out the best way to drag the beast back to camp. In the end, it took all three of us to get the makeshift sled to move that Malcolm had rigged from what was left of his trap.

While we walked, we chatted about the huge beast. None of us knew exactly what it was we were pulling. We just knew it was heavy and there was a lot of meat on it. We were sure it would be a welcome addition to whatever the other hunting parties brought in that day.

It took us a bit longer to get back to camp than we thought and we were not surprised to see the class packing up. Our instructor rushed over to us before we even pulled our kill past the edge of the trees.

"You're late! Where have you been? We have to head back right now! Sunset is closing in."

I rushed forward instinctively before I remembered the rope that I had looped over my shoulders and around my waist to help me keep hold of it. The weight of it jerked me back and I nearly lost my footing on the tightly packed snow.

We never did answer the instructor's question either, because a moment later, he chose to look behind us at the load on our makeshift sled.

"What. . . is. . . that?"

Adam was the first to answer him. "We don't really know. We were hoping you could tell us."

He began moving forward again. He knew as well as we did that we needed to get our catch to the gates. It would be difficult unless we kept moving.

Fortunately, the instructor jumped into action. Soon the others had finished packing up their gear. Once they had thrown their catches onto the makeshift sled with ours, they began to help us. With all twelve of us pulling, the load moved much faster and I breathed a sigh of relief. We would make it to the gates in plenty of time.

As we moved closer to the gates, I asked our instructor again about the identity of this huge beast. "Sir, don't you know what this thing is? Because none of us recognize it—and I don't remember seeing it in any of the training material."

Before he could answer, Jude spoke up. "I know what it is, but

I've only ever seen a picture of it. It's what they used to call a saber-toothed tiger. My papa was one of the original zookeepers when they came here. He had books with pictures of all the animals. Some of them didn't make it into the caves, so I'm not sure why they kept the books."

He shrugged before motioning to the load behind us. "This one though, I think was supposed to be dead a long time ago. I don't know how it came to be here."

Adam and Malcolm almost tripped when they stopped and looked back at Jude, while everyone else kept pulling the sled. It was difficult to figure if they were reacting to what he said or the fact that he had spoken at all. I knew I was shocked to hear him speaking as if he were certain of it.

Honestly, it didn't really matter to me how this huge beast had gotten here—or that it didn't belong. I was more surprised to hear such a long speech from the quietest boy in our class. I had never heard Jude speak much. He was obviously the quietest of us all. I would never have guessed he knew anything about animals.

He's just full of surprises.

When I turned around, I could see that we were almost to the gates and I felt myself relax.

We made it.

I hadn't realized how tense my muscles were until this

moment. I might have attributed it to the heavy load, but since everyone was pulling, it really wasn't that heavy anymore—and my muscles were relaxing one by one now.

I looked up as we went through the opening. On either side of us, there were guards. They stood there, weapons in hand, watching as we dragged our heavy load by them.

For a moment I thought they were going to stop us, but no one moved as we passed them and then kept going.

I let out a heavy breath of relief. We were safe. We were good. . . and we had a find that would hopefully thrill a lot of people.

As it turned out, our find did not thrill as many people as we were expecting. The veterinary section took charge of our kill just seconds after we pulled it through the gates.

I wondered at the time if someone from the wall had let them know when they saw us coming. It seemed more likely than thinking the vets just swooped in and snatched it out from under us.

Our instructor followed them to make sure that the credit for the find remained with our class.

By now I was sure he would give the credit to us all, not just Adam, Malcolm and me, but we were OK with that.

Two hours after we dragged the beast in, I almost wished we had not gotten the credit after all. We were all assailed by hordes of people from the entire complex.

Some of them wanted to congratulate us on the find, while others were angry we had turned it over to the veterinary staff.

Initially, I tried to defend our group, telling people who complained that the vet staff hadn't exactly given us a choice in the matter, but no one was in the mood to listen.

Jude surprised me again after a particularly rude man stormed away after my attempt at an explanation. “Don't let them get to you. People enjoy rumors a lot more than the truth. It’s more entertaining.”

All I could do was nod.

“Malcolm told me it was you who took that thing down. And with a single shot, too. Impressive.”

“Thanks.” I could feel heat creeping into my cheeks and I wasn't sure if I was more embarrassed over Jude being impressed by me, or by him knowing the truth about how we had gotten the kill.

I would have been willing to wager that Malcolm would tell the story as if he were the one to take down that enormous monster. To know that he was sharing the details—and so accurately—threw me off balance.

"If I were you, I would not mention it to anyone outside of our class. Some of these idiots are angry that we did not butcher the animal immediately and start passing out steaks, but honestly, I'm more worried about the others."

"What do you mean?" His words sent a shiver scuttling across the back of my neck like tiny fingers of ice.

"I mean that there are those who are angry for another reason."

"I still don't get why anyone is angry."

"I know, but just watch yourself." He turned and walked away. I was left standing there, watching his back as he strode purposefully across the room.

It didn't take long for me to come across someone from the group Jude had warned me about. They were different from everyone else. They were angry that we had killed such a rare specimen—and they weren't shy about showing their anger.

Several hours after we dragged the animal in, I was standing next to Adam and Anna in the hallway. We had just stowed our gear and were heading back when one of the people pounced on us. It was a woman, older than all of us, but still pretty young. She charged down the hall toward us, with venom in her eyes.

“What were you thinking? Don't you know what you've done? You've killed something that none of us may ever get the chance to see again.”

I was thrilled when Adam interrupted her. “Tell you what, next time you can go out there and get chased through the forest by something four times your size. Then we’ll see how you handle it.”

I had to stifle a laugh at the way her face looked. She was shocked!

“I'd actually like to see what you would have done. I guess you would have just let that rare specimen eat you.”

At that, every ounce of color drained out of her face. It happened so quickly, it was almost comical. She muttered something under her breath and turned to leave, dragging her feet as she went.

I almost felt bad for her as her shoulders slumped and she walked off with no enthusiasm left. Then I remembered the sound of that beast crashing through the forest and I didn't feel the least bit sorry after that.

ELEVEN

Arizona Caves

Year 45 A.E.

Day 119

Eleven hours after the veterinary service took the beast off our hands, I was sitting at the breakfast table across from my mother, watching the tears slip down her cheeks.

She didn't say a word. She wasn't eating. She sat there, sipping her coffee and silently crying. She didn't have to say anything—I knew she was thinking about what had happened the day before. I knew she was worried about me, but she was afraid to say anything to me.

I almost wished I had stayed in bed, but I knew we were scheduled to go out again today.

Apparently someone thought it would be a good idea to send us out more often since we'd brought in such a good haul.

Our instructor had come around after dinner and let everyone know that we needed to get an early start. I knew I really needed to get going. I didn't know what to say to her, but as I sat there, I felt myself getting more and more angry—and tense.

She knew what it was like outside the gates. She went out regularly with her own team. I wanted to yell at her. *Why did you even let me sign up for the stupid class?*

But I didn't. I just sat and watched her sip her coffee, watched the tears roll down one by one and wished there was something that I could say to help. I could tell her that I had been in the tree when the beast came through so I'd never really been in danger, but that wasn't true.

I had been in danger.

We had all been in danger—danger of getting trampled because even a tree wouldn't have stopped that beast. And we had also been in danger of not getting back to the compound in time. No one but the guards at the gate were supposed to know that, but since my Grandfather was a guard, I was certain he had told Mom exactly how close we had cut it coming in.

I could tell her that I was the one who shot the huge beast, so she would know I could handle myself, but I was sure it would come out sounding false to her.

It would sound like I was trying to calm her or make her feel better about me being out there. . . by telling her something that wasn't true.

I could remind her that no one had selected me for an internship and that I had been struggling to find my place in the compound all this time, but she already knew that. And she was already worried enough, she didn't need another reminder of how dangerous things could be for me outside the compound—or in it.

Since I couldn't say anything, I just sat and ate my breakfast.

Each bite felt like a rock going down my throat and each sip of tea, like acid, but I knew I would need my strength this morning, so I forced it all down. And then, just before I got up, I heard her voice. It was so quiet, I completely missed the first few words she said.

She obviously realized that because she cleared her throat and started over.

"The last words I spoke to your father were in anger. I'm not going to do that to you."

I looked up in shock. I hadn't noticed her beside me. At some point while I had been lost in my thoughts, she had gotten out of her chair and moved it over to me and now she sat right beside me.

"No matter what you do out there, I'm going to tell you I love you and that I support you one hundred percent. Because I do love you and I do support you. And I'm going to pray like crazy for you whenever you're out there."

She didn't say anything else, but when I got up and started to move past her, she reached for my hand. Then she pulled me back down to her and wrapped her arms around me. . . tight.

Her hot tears were pooling against my cheek and the pressure behind my own eyes increased. I was surprised at how tightly she held on to me. My relationship with Mom had felt strained since the day my father died and I had never figured out why until right now.

All this time, she had been trying to keep herself from being where she was right now, worried about me, worried that something would happen to me out there, that I would go the same way he had.

Her next words were barely a whisper, but I heard them easily because her mouth was so close to my ear.

"Just promise me you'll always come back to me."

A tear slipped down my cheek and I could feel a thickness closing up my throat; a barricade that would certainly make speech impossible.

With my new revelation, I wanted very much to tell her *of course I would always come back*, but something stopped me.

I really didn't want to worry her. I loved her so much. But I also did not want to lie to her. And that was the one thing I knew better than anyone that I couldn't promise her. As I fumbled for the right way to reassure her, it was all I could do to keep my tears from flowing freely now.

I wanted to promise her that I would never set foot outside the gates again. I wanted to tell her that nothing would ever happen to me. I wanted to find some way to ease her fears. But there was nothing I could say. There was no way I could promise any of those things. So I stayed right where I was and held her as tightly as I could, hoping that somehow she would be able to see my feelings through my actions.

The digital on the wall changed. Although I knew I had to leave soon, I could not make myself let go. And Mom certainly wasn't letting go. So there we stayed; her on the hard chair and me halfway between kneeling and standing, wrapped so tightly together and both with tears running silently down our cheeks.

I was surprised again when she let go. She did it slowly, but she was the one to let go. She untangled her arms from mine and then she looked at me and smiled.

"You go do what you have to do and I'll be here when you get back."

I slowly got to my feet and reached down to give her hand one more squeeze before moving to the hatch. I hefted my pack and retrieved my coat from the hook.

As I stood there, hand reaching out for the control panel, a thousand thoughts racing through my head.

What if something happens out there? I was almost killed yesterday. What if this is the last time I see her?

We have to feed everyone.

Yes, but is it really worth going—if it could possibly cost my life—or someone else's?

"I love you."

I heard the words, but I could tell she was having trouble getting them out. And that almost stopped me.

"Go on, now. You don't want to be late."

Only knowing how much worse it would be for her if I did not go to class. . . if I got into trouble over not showing up. . . made me move.

And just as I slid the hatch open, I whispered back. “I love you too, Mom.”

Her gasp followed me into the hall. I hadn't called her mom in several years. I hadn't been able to make myself do it for so long, yet I couldn't stop myself now.

I looked back at her before I shut the hatch—and I was glad I did. She was sitting with a really big smile on her face. There were still tears and they might even be coming a little faster now, but she was smiling through them. And she nodded at me.

That nod gave me all the courage I needed to shut the hatch and turn to go down the hall toward the front of the complex.

TWELVE

Arizona Caves

Year 45 A.E.

Day 142

All of my worry was for nothing. All her worry was for nothing. Weeks went by. We ventured out six more times—and we brought in some impressive kills, but none of us had seen anything like that rampaging beast again.

Twice we had tried following the exact path Adam had taken. . . then we skirted around it another two times, but no one saw anything remotely like that giant monster.

After we had come in from our fourth extra hunting trip, we heard the veterinary team had finally confirmed what Jude had told us that day while we were dragging the enormous thing toward the compound. They confirmed that, although it was not precisely the same as the creatures in their files, it was a close enough match that they had officially classified it a saber-toothed tiger.

Another three days had passed before they'd finally released it to the kitchen. . . well, pieces of it anyway.

But it was enough of a triumph that the chancellor had decided it warranted a celebration. This called for something special. . . plans soon got under way for a complex-wide party! It had been more than a few years since one had been held. For many of us, it was a brand new experience.

I remembered my father telling me about the last big celebration in the caves that he remembered. He had talked about it again and again when I was a child, because it had occurred on the very night I was born. Even though it had nothing to do with my birth, he'd always felt especially fond of retelling the story, because of the coincidence of timing.

It had been his favorite story. . . and mine as well. . . when I was growing up. He and my mother had celebrated in their own way that night—not only because of my birth, but due to the fact that I was their second child. That was a miracle to them because of the law that had just been put into effect the day before; limiting families to two children.

From what I knew of that time in the caves—and I didn't know much because nobody liked to talk about it—it had been a very scary time for a lot of people. The weather had been exceptionally cold for a very long time that year, so cold that the few parties who were actually able to get out to hunt had found nothing. Absolutely nothing.

Horrific storms had raged on for months. The animals had either been in hiding or still in hibernation.

Supplies had trickled down to the most basic rations and even those were stretched thin. A new law had been put into effect a month before I was born, stating that no family could have more than two children. If I had been their third, my mother's pregnancy would have been terminated.

Everyone had been on edge, because of the new law. . . and because at that point, supplies had been tight for weeks.

Then, two days before I was born, the weather had cleared and the hunting parties immediately headed out. Because so many animals were coming out of hibernation at the same time, all the groups came back with full loads and the people in the caves breathed a sigh of relief. It just happened to be the night I was born when the chancellor declared a celebration.

Just after I celebrated my second birthday, that chancellor had died from a heart attack and his second-in-command had stepped into the office.

My father had told me many times. . . this was when things in the caves had started to drastically change.

Since I had never really known any other way, I'd always taken his word for it. My father had worked in the first chancellor's office. They had worked closely on many things and my father had considered him to be a personal friend.

I had thought for a long time that my father's affection for the former chancellor might be part of why he seemed to be against the new chancellor. But now I found myself seeing things from a different perspective.

Was there more to it?

Could there be something to what my father told me all those years about the stark differences between the two men?

THIRTEEN

Arizona Caves

Year 45 A.E.

Day 143

As we trekked through the forest, I thought about all of the things that were beginning to unfold. Between the secrets my father had trusted me with—and the things I had discovered on my own—troubling images were starting to form and I found myself questioning everything I had ever taken at face value.

Nothing felt the same anymore. Nothing felt normal. . . familiar. . . safe.

Looking around at the others in class, I reminded myself to keep my expression blank. I couldn't let on that I suspected anything was wrong with the caves. Our family especially. . . could not afford to draw attention to itself. It was difficult, but I pushed the heavy thoughts out of my head and focused on what was going on around me.

There was a new layer of snow—at least a foot deep—or more.

We had been out the day before, but when everyone tasted the mouth-watering feast the kitchens had prepared, they had all made requests that we hunt for more of this type of meat. So here we were, hunting again.

We were wearing snowshoes on this trip because of the deep, thick snow. Our instructor had actually gone back to get snowshoes for everyone when he saw how deep the snow was. We hadn't gotten twenty feet from the gate when he told us to stop and wait for him. Then he'd turned and rushed back in.

Not quite ten minutes later he had come back out, pulling a sled full of the weirdest contraptions I had ever seen. He told us the master-of-arms had been waiting for him—with a smirk on her face. Somehow she'd known exactly what he needed before he had even come back into the cave. The sled was prepped and packed, waiting for him when he arrived.

“Spooky. . . is she not?”

I looked up in surprise. The comment had come from Jude. I

hadn't heard more than two words from him since the incident with the tiger, but he spoke easily now—almost as if we had been in the midst of a conversation—while he strapped the odd "shoes" to the bottoms of his heavy boots. He looked very competent, as if he'd used them before.

"Wow Jude, you look like you know what you're doing. Mind giving me a few pointers?"

He looked up with a grin and I was surprised again.

I had seen him smile. . . perhaps one other time. He wasn't particularly unhappy—not that I knew anyway—he just wasn't one to smile. His smile seemed different somehow, carefree, almost like he was just a kid out for some fun.

"Absolutely. I can show you how to work them."

I watched him as he finished fastening them to his heavy boots.

"What about after that? Will you show me how to use them? Something tells me they aren't as easy to use as they are to fasten."

He laughed. "Yes. I will show you. They are not so difficult as you may think." And he moved over to begin fastening the ones given to me to my boots.

"I have used them only once myself. It was a gift from my papa. He took me outside for my birthday and the snow was very deep so we needed these. He used them many times. He showed me." He took a breath and shook his head a little before going on.

"Before the caves, he was a bit of an explorer, my papa. It was good. He was a help to the people when they first came out of the caves."

It took me a minute to say anything back. That was definitely the longest speech I had ever heard out of him. I wasn't sure what to say since I was fairly certain his "papa" was gone now —like my own father.

"Do you want to hear more about that?"

I nodded. I still couldn't think of what to say, but more than that, I wanted him to keep talking. It was difficult to decide if I was enjoying the way he spoke—or the cadence and tone of his voice. It was different from anyone else I knew.

"It's OK. I miss him still." He was looking down at the snowshoe he had attached to my left boot, so I couldn't see his face, but his voice was sad.

"He would not be happy with me if he knew I mourn him still." He laughed a little at that. "He would tell me to let it go and live! He was that way, always. . . so alive. I think perhaps it might be easier for me to let him go because he helped me to live so much more."

He looked over at me then. "You lost your father, too. Yes? Were you very young?"

Numbly, I nodded. I was almost ready to admit to myself that my enjoyment with listening to Jude had less to do with the way he spoke—and more to do with the young man himself. I struggled to think of something to say. . . anything that would make sense, but when I opened my mouth to speak, somehow what came out was not at all what I intended.

"Why do you talk like that?" Immediately I slapped my hand over my mouth. Then a second later, I tried again, speaking through the hand I still held over my mouth. "I'm sorry."

But he was laughing—not in an annoyed way or like he was making fun—more like he was delighted with me.

"I really am sorry. That's not what I meant to say at all."

"Do not worry yourself. I am very much accustomed to it. It is one thing I have from my papa. He came from what they used to call the Ukraine. He came to America secretly as a young man with his family."

He laughed again. "You should have heard *his* accent. He. . ."

He didn't say anything else for a moment and I stayed quiet. I was beginning to wonder if I would be able to enjoy listening to anyone else speaking. Compared to the lilt of Jude's tone and the unique way he strung his words together, the way everyone else spoke seemed awfully ordinary—and boring.

"He always told me it was his first great adventure. It gave him a thirst for adventure, and for learning. When he came to this country, he worked very hard to learn the English so he could explore the country with little difficulty." The smile slipped a little, but he kept talking. . . and I kept listening.

"He had many adventures. He told me many wonderful stories. I believe it is why I sound so much like him." And then the smile was there again, lighting up his face.

Clearly, he had really loved his papa. It made me think of the relationship I'd had with my father. It was something beautiful. It gave me a whole new insight to Jude.

I looked at his face as he fastened the last straps on my right snowshoe. The smile made him so much more approachable.

I hadn't known him before our class, so I couldn't be sure he hadn't always been this way. Perhaps the newness of the class had changed him, but it seemed more like I was seeing a whole new side to him I had not seen before.

Once he finished with my snowshoes, he stood, offering me his hand as he did. When I placed my hand in his, I noticed right away that his grip was strong and firm, although his skin was a little rough from the hard work we all had to do. . . and from the cold, too. The weather and the cold temperatures did a number on everyone's skin, but especially those of us who worked outside.

He continued to hold my hand, helping me to find my balance on the unfamiliar new devices. Standing or moving around on snowshoes was something I would have to work at awhile to get used to. I was very thankful for his help to steady me.

I looked around at the rest of the class. There were only a couple of others standing and they did not look very steady. The rest were either still trying to figure out how to fasten the huge things to their feet or they were on the ground in various awkward positions. The instructor was going from person to person, explaining how to fasten the myriad of buckles and straps.

If it weren't for Jude's help, I would have been in the same position, waiting for the instructor to help me. It was a very humbling experience—to find something that I had no experience with—and no natural skill for it.

My next words were very quiet, mostly because I didn't want to draw attention to either of us, but I also wanted to make sure he knew just how much I appreciated what he was doing for me.

"Thank you."

He nodded and then inclined his head in an odd way, almost like a little bow. I only knew what a bow was because I had seen my father do it with my mother when I was very little and I had asked him what it was.

I could remember watching them dance around our tiny living area. My father would always stand up and bow in a very dramatic way to my mother. Then he would take her hand and spin her in very close to him. Then he would spin her out as far as he could reach, and they would start doing all these wonderful twists and turns in the small, open space.

It had been wondrous to watch and I had always held the memory close so that I didn't forget it. They had made the dancing look so fluid and beautiful. It was memories like that one that made me think about how much I missed him.

"You are most welcome."

What he said next surprised me. I hadn't thought anyone paid that much attention to me. I certainly never thought he had paid attention to me, but apparently I was wrong.

"I would not want you to look silly. You are always so graceful."

"Thank you." The words came out automatically, and I almost wished I could snatch them back. I certainly didn't always feel graceful.

The thought occurred to me that Jude had been watching me. How else would he be able to say "always"?

I wanted to speak. . . to say more, but it felt like my tongue was glued to the roof of my mouth.

When I felt the heat rush into my cheeks, I looked down. I was beginning to notice a strange feeling from our connected hands. I liked having him hold my hand, and I was surprised to discover that it wasn't just because he was keeping me from falling, but because it felt nice. It was warm. . . and comforting.

Out here, surrounded by ice and snow and cold wind, it was shocking to discover an unexpected warmth.

What is this? What is going on here? I didn't even know what to think, where to start.

Six weeks ago, I hadn't even known Jude. Three weeks ago, I had thought he was a quiet, normal young man who liked to keep to himself. Now I could see that he had unexpected layers. He knew things that were beautiful. . . even poetic.

I had discovered a new depth to him. He was full of compassion. He was full of warmth—and I liked it.

I like him.

And that thought confused me. Of course I liked him. I liked everybody.

Well. . . not everybody, but most.

I looked up at his face to find him watching me. There was something different in his eyes, something I hadn't seen before—something confusing, which sent another rush of heat to my cheeks.

Uncertainty and confusion rolled around in my head. I had no idea what to think about such intense thoughts pushing their way through my confused mind. I had never experienced such a feeling—and didn't know how to explain it. My legs grew weak and I felt breathless.

I looked away from his face and made myself breathe in and out very slowly—big, deep breaths.

Satisfied there was nothing wrong with me, I looked back at him—and it happened again. My breath stuck in my throat and I noticed the warmth now spreading through my chest.

The spell was suddenly broken when a snowball flew past my shoulder and hit Jude in the face.

Looking around, I saw Adam less than ten feet away—laughing! It wasn't hard to figure out who the culprit was. He'd obviously gotten the hang of using snowshoes. In fact, he was already leaning down and packing together another snowball.

Jude gave my hand a squeeze before letting go and leaning down to make his own snowball. I watched him to see what he was doing with his body and his feet and tried to imitate him so I could make a snowball, too.

I certainly didn't want to just be a target!

I was surprised to find that standing and leaning were much easier than I had expected. It was certainly easier than trying to walk through the deep snow, sinking down with each step. Before I could stand back up, a snowball hit me in the rear and

I looked around, without standing up, to see who had thrown it.

Anna was still sitting in the snow, but she had a big smile on her face and a small pile of snowballs next to her. She laughed as she sent them flying at each one of us in turn. Several snowballs hit her in return as she sat there, but she never stopped laughing.

I stood back up just as another snowball came my direction and it hit me square in the chest with a thick splat. I couldn't be sure who threw it because snowballs were now coming and going in every direction.

Shrieks of laughter and surprise sounded all around me as people hit their targets—and were hit by others.

I looked over at the instructor. No one had dared hit him yet and he wasn't joining in, but he looked amused at the scene in front of him.

He stood there with his arms crossed over his chest, a slight smile playing at the corners of his mouth. I couldn’t help myself; I flung the snowball in my hand at him as hard as I could, before turning the other direction and taking off as quickly as possible, still struggling a little with the unfamiliar snowshoes.

As I went, I was pelted with snowballs from all around as I launched snowballs at random people, laughing all the time. A second later, someone bumped me and we both went tumbling into the snow.

My face hit first, but it hit a soft mound of snow and sunk down into it. I was still laughing as I rolled over, trying to keep from sinking too far into the soft snow. Looking over, I realized it was Jude who had hit me. He must have been right at my back the whole time. He was sitting beside me in the snow, laughing with everybody else while a few snowballs still flew around the group.

We sat there laughing, while watching the last few sail across the open space in front of us, but there were no more coming in our direction.

It wasn't more than a second or two before the last one fell with a splat. Everyone around us was either still sitting or had dropped down into the thick snow. Mostly they were still laughing, but it had quieted a little and I could see that the snowball fight was over.

I looked around at all of the faces. Everyone looked happy, more relaxed than I had seen anyone in weeks. . . until I looked at Alan. He had a smile on his face, but I could see, even from so far away that it was very tight at the edges and there was a hardness in his eyes.

He looked almost angry as he stood there, looking at everyone around him. Then, as I watched him, the look changed. It softened, but it still didn't look natural. It looked forced, like he was relaxing the muscles in his face one at a time.

It was almost a bit frightening to watch. I felt the hairs stand up on the back of my neck and I purposely made myself look away. Beside me, Jude put his hand on my arm.

"Are you all right? I did not hurt you? I was not trying to collide with you. I should have been watching better where I was going."

He looked very concerned and I almost wanted to say something to him about what I had just seen, but before I could open my mouth to speak, my father's words echoed in my head about how important it was to keep little things to myself.

"Not to keep secrets, but to protect those around us."

And I knew it would be a bad idea to tell Jude anything, especially right now. So I turned to him and forced a smile of my own, trying for playful, hoping that would diffuse the tension that was suddenly between us in the air

"Yeah I'm good, at least for someone who just got knocked over by a brick wall."

For a second, I thought he was going to get upset, but then he must have noticed the slight upturn of my lips and realized that I was kidding.

"Well, as long as you will be all right." Then he laughed and I breathed a sigh of relief. Hopefully he hadn't noticed how tight my own smile was.

Before I could worry about it any further, the instructor was calling us all together. I looked around at the group again.

Some of the others were still struggling a bit with their snowshoes, but there were others who looked completely comfortable in them by now.

I felt like I'd gotten the hang of them, too. Jude had taken my hand to help me up out of the snow and he had kept hold of it while we moved back to the group, but had let go when we reached the group.

I wanted to wonder what that meant, but I was still thinking of the look on Alan's face. There was no reason I could think of for him to look that way.

Granted, I hadn't been watching everyone the entire time, being hit by snowy projectiles and working to gain my balance, but I'd looked around at everyone before being distracted by Alan. There was nothing in those moments that should have angered Alan.

Unless there was something I didn't know about, something that had looked perfectly innocent to me, but not to Alan. Maybe someone else had been doing something that especially bothered Alan and I just hadn't noticed it.

There was a tiny part of me that wanted to think it wasn't anything like that. But even while I tried to convince myself that there must be a simple explanation for it, I didn't really believe it.

The instructor's voice distracted me. When I looked over at him, I saw that he was putting us into groups, and some of them were already heading out to start hunting. I tried to let go of the feeling I had about Alan, but it stayed in the back of my mind.

I was grateful when the instructor finally got to me. He would send me off hunting and I could focus on that. Hopefully it would help.

“Eve. You've been out with Malcolm and Adam every time since you three bagged that tiger. Why don't we see if we can get more luck changing up the groups a bit? This time, you and Jude go with Anna.”

“Yes sir.” It was Jude who spoke, while I looked over at Anna and back to him.

I should have been relieved not to be paired with Alan, but I couldn't help the skittering that went up and down my spine. I thought back to what had been happening before the snowball fight.

Did I really want to be all alone with Jude and Anna out in the forest?

It's not like I really have a choice.

The thought just popped into my head. But I knew it was right. The instructor didn't care what had been happening before. He just wanted a good catch to take back to the complex.

Anna slowly moved over to us, obviously still trying to get the hang of the snowshoes. She was doing very well. I was happy about that. It was good to know she wouldn't slow us down. As I started to think about the hunt ahead, everything else was pushed to the back of my mind as I began thinking about strategy.

I was so focused; it surprised me when Jude's voice interrupted my thoughts.

"I can see the wheels turning in that head of yours. You have an idea already, yes?"

His words didn't really give much of a clue as to what he was thinking and that worried me a little.

Malcolm and Adam had been perfectly happy to let me lead when it had been the three of us. None of us had made a production of telling everyone who had taken down the tiger, but they both knew it was me and the three of us had just fallen into a natural rhythm of hunting.

Clearly this would be different though. It made me unsure of what to say or do.

Is Jude used to being the leader? Will he have trouble with me leading. . . with me thinking strategy?

“They are still turning. You are worried now about what I say. Allow me to rephrase please. I can see that you have an idea. Would you share it with us?”

Looking up at him, I could see there was no anger or irritation clouding his features.

He means it. . . good.

“I do have an idea actually. I don't want to step on anybody's toes, but I guess I'm just used to leading.”

Too late, I realized what I'd said. I had just told both of them that Malcolm and Adam were both happy to let a woman lead them. Jude was smiling, but it looked like he was trying not to laugh.

“What I meant to say was. . .” And I stumbled over my words again. I was trying so hard not to say the wrong thing.

Both of them began to laugh now.

“Oh, forget it.” I looked at the two of them. They were laughing. . . hard now. Anna had sat down—or maybe she even fallen down—and Jude was bent over, gripping his knees in an effort to stay upright.

They obviously weren't upset and they weren't bothered at all by anything I had said. They were enjoying it far too much.

And in that moment, I knew exactly what to do.

I reached over and gave Jude's shoulder a shove—a hard one—and he toppled over sideways. A look of surprise crossed his features as he fell, and then he was laughing again. I stood there, hands on hips, waiting for them to get serious again.

I never saw his foot coming. He swept his leg behind mine and knocked my legs out from under me—and I was tumbling into the snow beside him.

I would have landed on my face, but he reached out and cushioned my fall. I felt something hit my lip as I fell. It felt like little stars of pain shot out from the spot and I tasted blood. I was quick to pull my lip inside my mouth. I knew blood out here was not a good idea.

And suddenly he was not laughing anymore. He was jumping up and running for his pack—or as close to running as he could do with the bulky snowshoes strapped to his feet.

Thankfully, it was only a few feet away. Snow sprayed me as he skidded to a stop next to me and then he was yanking zippers and throwing things out of his pack to get to the first-aid kit buried at the bottom.

I had a moment to think that whoever had organized the packs needed a lesson in the order of essentials, but then Jude was holding my face and talking to me, almost yelling in his distress.

“Let me see your lip. Hurry!”

So I stuck my lip out and a slightly cold spray hit it. Immediately it changed and I felt something warm where he had just sprayed, which seemed weird since it was so cold.

His hands returned to either side of my face as he looked at my lip, and he breathed a sigh of relief.

“We got it in time. I am so sorry. Once again, I should have been more cautious. I was not watching closely enough. Will you be all right?”

I wanted to laugh. The absolute ridiculousness of the last few minutes was starting to sink in as I answered Jude.

“I'm fine. Thanks.” It might have been fun to leave him dangling, but it didn't seem fair. After all, he'd taken care of my lip.

Granted he had caused it. . . but he'd also fixed it.

“That was quick thinking. Great job.”

I took advantage of his distraction, and smooshed a snowball into his face, laughing as he sputtered.

Anna was laughing behind us. “Yeah, you had that one coming.”

Jude leaned away to wipe the snow off his face and I took the opportunity to get up before he could retaliate. Then I moved over to where Anna stood and we waited for Jude to join us.

He sat there in the snow with his head hanging down. I couldn't be sure, but it looked like he was laughing again.

"I couldn't resist."

When he stayed where he was, I started to worry just a little, but he finally raised his head and we could see that he was smiling. It was only another second or two, before he bounced up and moved over to us.

"Since we have had our fun. . ." He aimed a look at me—and the breath caught in my throat again. "Let us get serious now, yes?"

I could only nod in response. Anna must have nodded, because he went on.

"Good. Now, I am willing to go along with whatever plan you have since your team has been the most successful in our class."

I nodded again, more business-like this time. My head was already thinking ahead, plotting out our course and the steps we should take to set a successful trap.

"OK. So here's what we do. . ."

FOURTEEN

Arizona Caves

Year 45 A.E.

Day 147

I was surprised to see so many nods aimed in my direction as I walked through the caves. Everyone seemed to know who I was now and it was unexpected—and a little bit embarrassing.

Our class had earned a fame of sorts with that one kill.

We had given the scientists something new to study, the other hunters something to aspire to and the other residents something to celebrate.

Unfortunately, we had also done something I had worked hard from day one in the class to not do. We had drawn attention to ourselves.

It didn't seem to matter that our hunting trips since had turned up nothing out of the ordinary—just normal animals in normal quantities. It didn't seem to matter that bringing in that monster had been a complete fluke to begin with.

It only mattered that we were getting more than our fair share of attention.

Unfortunately, there were more than a few people in the caves who did not take kindly to that.

Several times, twice just in the last few days, different students had turned up in class with a bruise or a black eye or a split lip.

Lily had missed class completely for almost a week because someone had put her in the infirmary, which also meant she had missed two hunts and the impromptu snowball fight.

Ironic that Mom was worried about me going out. Lately it feels a lot more dangerous inside than out.

It certainly explained the reason we had all felt such a need to engage in so much silliness on our last hunt. We were all a bit wound up.

I had thought—before Lily had ended up in the infirmary—that it was mostly due to the tension and the expectation resting on us to find another tiger, but that one incident had made it clear to me that finding another tiger was the least of our worries.

As one of the smallest in the class, I had taken to spending a lot more time working out and exercising. I had also started to carry Dad's hunting knife with me everywhere.

It didn't take long for me to find out that I was not the only one. Our instructor informed us one morning that we would be allowed a special consideration due to our training, just before he passed out the hunting knives that we usually returned with our other weapons when we came back inside.

And it was a good thing, too.

On my way to the evening meal, just four days after our hunt that had started with a snowball fight, my feet were knocked out from under me unexpectedly.

With no snow to cushion my fall, I twisted my body at the last second and rolled, which turned out to be the best thing I could have done because I heard someone's foot thud onto the floor a few feet from where I ended up, right where my face would have been if I hadn't moved.

Because I had moved, that foot missed its target. And because I was not there to be the target, the person over-balanced and ended up tumbling forward onto the floor.

Had I been any of the other students, I would have turned and attacked. But I wasn't one of the others. Grandad had always stressed that a person should avoid a fight if it was at all possible—so I did what he'd taught me.

I ran.

I had already rolled a good distance away so I kept rolling and used the momentum to get to my feet easily and quickly. Then I sprinted toward the main hall, keeping my body as low to the ground as I could.

I didn't encounter anyone in the halls for several turns, but then, around the fourth corner I turned, I smacked into someone. When we collided, I heard a loud crack and a thud as they fell backwards into the wall.

Without really thinking, I dropped into a fighting stance. I'd already been knocked down and they would have done a lot more then, that if I hadn't evaded them and run for it. I was not about to be taken out by someone who was late to the ambush.

“What! Who is there!” A very angry voice came out of the dark of the corner. Oddly enough, even without being able to see the person *and* with the voice being slightly muffled, I knew who it was.

“Jude, what are you doing down here?”

“Eve? You ran into me? What is going on?”

“Jude, I'm sorry. Someone knocked my legs out from under me and I ran for it. This time I guess I should have been paying better attention to where I was going. Are you all right?”

My eyes were starting to adjust to the darkness and I could see him a little more clearly so I reached out to help him up off the floor.

"Someone attacked you? Where are they?" The tone of his voice worried me. He sounded like he was after blood.

"Jude, please let it go?" He started to shake off my hand and I held tighter. "Please. Come on, let's get you to the infirmary and see if your nose is broken."

"Fine. This time." He still sounded angry, but I had no way of knowing if it was due to his injury or the fact that I'd stopped him from going after my attacker.

He lifted a hand to his face and then muttered something I couldn't understand. It didn't sound like a good word.

As we moved into the light, I could see blood gushing from his nose. I wanted to apologize again, but after a look at his expression, I knew that would be a bad idea.

The irony was not lost on me. Whoever it was that had attacked me had been going for my blood—and now I had smashed Jude's nose while running away from my attacker.

"How did you know it was me? You could not see." His voice was still muffled, and as we moved into brighter areas, it looked like bruises were beginning to form under both of his eyes.

"I recognized your voice. You have a very distinctive voice." He looked at me then—and there was a strange expression on his face. I tried to tell myself it was simply the pain from his nose, but I couldn't quite convince myself.

"Still, in the dark, it wouldn't be surprising if you had thought I was another attacker."

I cringed a little. That was exactly what I had thought. Of course, I hadn't hit him because I thought he was an attacker, but still. . .

"Actually I did at first. I hadn't gone very far and I thought you might be an attacker who was coming from behind me. Until I heard your voice, that is." I closed my eyes as embarrassment washed over me. I hoped he wouldn't hold it against me.

"In that case, I am glad you did recognize my voice. I would hate to think what you could have done to me if I hadn't spoken."

I thought I could hear a trace of amusement, but I couldn't be sure. He was really hard to understand at the moment.

"You know, I ran into you, because I was trying to get away. I wasn't trying to hurt you." I gritted my teeth as I said it, hoping he would hear the truth in it and not pick out what I wasn't saying.

After all, he hadn't *seen* me drop into my fighting stance. . . or I didn't think he had anyway.

"That is good point. However, the fact remains—you could have done serious damage."

I let out a huff of breath. He really had been watching me. *He isn't fooled at all.*

"I have never thought that you learned the things you know only from our class. You do things too well—with very little instruction." He stopped for a second. Even in the dark corridor, I could see him looking at me and waiting for me to confirm what he said.

"Someone has taught you much more than you care to let others know. I do not understand why you would hide your skill, unless you are afraid of being a target."

I gasped. He was so much smarter than everyone thought. He knew exactly what I had done all along—and was still doing even now. How he knew was still a bit of a mystery, but it was obvious he had been paying more attention to me than I knew or he couldn't have known enough to make those assumptions.

So he had been watching me—all along.

Is that creepy? Should I be worried?

He had saved my skin our last time out and he had helped me when he really didn't have to. He hadn't given me a hard time about ramming into him and I'd most likely broken his nose.

Was I just being paranoid—or was I right to worry?

He started walking again. I hurried to catch up to him. He would have to explain to whoever was on duty in the infirmary about what had happened to him and they would most likely insist I get checked out, too.

It might not be a terrible idea.

My head had hit the floor pretty hard when my legs got knocked out from under me and I was aware of a pain just under my ribs, too. I didn't remember hitting my ribs anywhere, but maybe it was from where I had collided with Jude. When I'd slammed into him, every part of my body had hit every part of his body so it was entirely possible.

We didn't come across anyone else on our way to the infirmary. When we walked in, we were both surprised to see Lily sitting on one of the beds. Before we had a chance to ask her why she was there, the nurse rushed into the room. As we walked past her bed, I couldn't help but notice a white bandage wrapped around Lily's leg.

Poor Lily. Who is doing this to her?

The nurse was not at all sympathetic to either of us. She behaved like it was our fault we had shown up in her nice clean infirmary and it made me feel very chastised. Even if it was sort of my fault that Jude was here, I hadn't done anything to get attacked. It wasn't like we did it on purpose to ruin her night. It was more than a little annoying.

Added to that, my ribs were really starting to hurt and Jude's nose had not stopped bleeding or even slowed down that I could tell. So it wasn't like we could have done anything else.

She grudgingly worked on us, taking care of Jude first, since he was bleeding everywhere. She took hold of his fingers and put them on his nose in a very specific place and the bleeding slowed down. After just a few seconds it stopped completely, while the nurse went about the business of cleaning him up. She wiped down his face and then started poking and prodding.

I was watching the whole thing and I noticed him wince several times, but he never screamed or yelled. He just sat there, letting her poke and prod and pull on his injured face.

When she was done, she went to the end of the hall, then through a doorway, without a word to either of us. He looked over at me and smiled. I noticed a strange color around his nose, but I couldn't tell if it was dried blood or the start of a bruise. I guessed it was a bruise, because his nose was definitely broken.

After about ten minutes, the nurse came back and dragged me off to a different room to have my ribs checked. It surprised me when she told me to take my clothes off, but she explained that she had to use a scanner and having clothes on apparently made the images fuzzy. I felt more than little weird, but I did as she asked.

The scanner showed that I had cracked a couple of ribs. Surprisingly, she took care of it in a matter of seconds—without hurting me. Sooner than expected, we were making our way back to Jude.

He was talking to Lily when we came back in. They both stopped talking when we came back in. Jude was still sitting with his fingers where the nurse had placed them. Lily was reading a book, looking like she was trying to make a point of not showing that she had just been in deep discussion with Jude. It made me wonder what they had been talking about, but I could take a hint, so I didn't say anything to either of them.

I walked over and sat on the bed next to Jude. The nurse followed behind me, stopping in front of Jude. Looking for signs of bleeding, she told him he could move his fingers away from his nose.

He did as she asked. I watched, expecting the bleeding to start up again. I could tell Jude was waiting, too, but thankfully no blood flowed. His nose looked a little funny—and he looked like someone had given him two black eyes.

I had never seen someone with a freshly-broken nose so I'd had no idea what to expect, but I felt even worse about the whole thing now, sitting there next to him, clearly not hurting as much as he was. And he obviously picked up on it, too.

Once the nurse walked out of the room again, he spoke up.

“I can see you are blaming yourself. Don't. This was an accident. You know I am right. Anyway, we can both blame this on the idiots who attacked you.”

“But. . .”

He held up a hand before I could finish. “No buts. There is no need for anyone to know that you were attacked somewhere else, right?”

And I had to smile. He had come up with the perfect solution.

No one would guess what had happened—and he wouldn't look weak to the rest of the class.

It was brilliant.

He was brilliant.

FIFTEEN

Arizona Caves

Year 45 A.E.

Day 152

I looked over at Jude as we fought our way through the snow. We were outside again, but not for hunting this time—it was for additional training.

The snow was deep, but for several reasons the instructor had decided we wouldn't be wearing snowshoes on this outing. I figured it was mostly due to the training.

We weren't hunting, so we didn't have to be super quiet. On this trip, we were supposed to be learning more about the area.

So far, it didn't feel very productive, but it was interesting. This was an area I knew I needed more experience with. Grandad might have been able to teach me the skills he had learned, but he hadn't been able to come up with a good enough reason to take me outside. Once we began going outside, one thing I had discovered was that the pictures in our books did not do the trees or the animals justice.

We were not broken up into small groups on this trip. We were all together, moving through the forest. I was secretly thrilled to find that Jude ended up on my right.

His nose was healing nicely, but it looked like it might end up a little crooked once it did. The nurse had said that she could do a procedure to straighten it, but it was very painful. I couldn't be sure if it was the possibility of more pain that stopped him or the thought that he would look tougher with a slightly crooked nose, but whatever the reason, he had opted for no procedure and now his nose was healing—crooked.

The bruises around his eyes were fading, but they looked mostly green, yellow and nasty.

It seemed like I had come out better on the deal all around. Whatever that nurse had done to my ribs had fixed them completely. I had no other signs of injury and Jude had attributed all of his injuries to the attackers I had run from.

It worked out well. He hadn't technically lied to anyone—though it certainly felt that way to me. And, because everyone had already come to their own conclusion, he got to be a hero. Everyone just assumed he had jumped in and saved me from the attackers.

It had been all anyone had talked about for days.

So here we all were, out in the woods. I was certain I wasn't the only one who had a strong feeling that we were out here to keep us out of the caves. Yes, we were learning a lot, but we could easily have done this quick lesson on any number of other hunting trips.

I could read between the lines.

Each of us had been attacked while in the caves. Adam had almost had his throat slit. Lily's left leg was broken in four places, Anna had been badly beaten and Malcolm had been bashed over the head with some horrible weapon that was covered in sharp points.

He was actually still in the infirmary because of all the bleeding. But our instructor had assured us he would not be alone.

I didn't even want to think about what the attackers would have done to me if they'd managed to keep me there with them. And if being out here learning things kept us safe, I was all for it.

Cold was better than dead any day. And it was nice to be out of the complex. I hadn't realized until we started going out, how confining the caves felt. It was probably when I compared it to the wide open spaces outside of the gates that I noticed. But it didn't change the fact that the caves suddenly felt very small.

Several hours later, the class was still together, but everyone had once again drifted apart into smaller groups. I looked over at Jude and smiled; I couldn't help myself. Suddenly I felt great.

I was thrilled to be outside. I was thrilled to be in the forest. I was thrilled not to be stuck indoors. I didn't even care anymore about the attack or the conclusions everyone had jumped to about them.

I felt free and happy and I suddenly felt like I needed to be a lot nicer to Jude.

He had saved me. . . in a way. He hadn't told anyone about my clumsiness running around that corner. And he hadn't told anyone about my extra skills, so I didn't have to worry about being more of a target, although I really felt like we should all band together a bit more with all the attacks coming from within. So, since he had saved me, I owed him.

In that mood, I walked over to him and looped my arm through his as we walked. He looked down at me, confusion all over his face.

"You are no longer angry with me then?" There was a bit of a smile pulling at the corner of his mouth, but it looked like he was holding it back.

"I never was angry with you. I'm just not comfortable with lies. And it's silly to say that because I've sort of been lying all this time anyway. I've held back how good I am at everything we've been learning." And I looked up at him as he made a little hum in his throat.

"So it was really unfair of me to ever snip at you about how we told the story. It was clearly the best solution and the best way to keep us both safe. So, thanks." I kept my arm tucked through his as we continued to move through the forest.

"It was a bit unorthodox, I admit. What is the phrase. . . *it seemed like a good idea at the time.*"

I nodded, because I did know.

We kept walking, but we were moving slowly through the trees. He hadn't objected to me holding onto his arm, so I hadn't let go. There was something I had wanted to ask him for a while and I was trying to gather my courage. Even though we were outside, none of the other students were close by, so now was the perfect time. We probably took another hundred steps before I finally got up the nerve to blurt it out.

"I have a weird question for you." He didn't say anything, so I kept going. "And please don't get mad, but. . . well, you remember that day we had our snowball fight—" I left it hanging, looking up at him.

He was nodding. The expression on his face was puzzled, but not guarded, so I pushed on.

"Were you going to kiss me?" I rushed on without really giving him a chance to answer. "We were standing there after you helped me up with my snowshoes. We were standing kind of close—and it just seemed like you had that look, like you were going to lean in and kiss me. I'm asking because that idiot Adam hit you with a snowball right then, and you didn't kiss me and, well, I was left wondering, and I really wanted to know." I stopped then to take a breath.

He didn't say anything right away. I wondered if I had misjudged the situation or if I had said the wrong thing or if I had unintentionally offended him or what.

I sneaked a look at him and I realized he was staring at me. He was really staring—and there was a very intense look in his eyes. He was looking at me the same way he had looked at me that day. And suddenly I felt the heat again. We were standing there, surrounded by snow, but we could have been right next to a crackling fire. There was that much warmth filling me.

He reached up and brushed my hair away from my face where it fell out of my hood, and then he put his hands on either side of my face and I looked at his lips and tried to swallow, but I was unsuccessful. It was like there was something stuck in my throat, perhaps a ball of nerves.

I looked back up at his face and his eyes were even more intense than they had been a moment ago. He was staring into my eyes and I tried to look away, but I couldn't seem to make my eyes move this time. So I looked at him—and he looked at me—and he began to move his head, his face coming closer to mine.

And we heard a shout behind us.

"Hey guys! You've got to come look at this! Hurry! You won't believe what we found!"

Jude turned his head in the direction the shout had come from. The look in his eyes was still very intense, but somehow it was also different.

"One of these days. . ." He let the words hang in the air.

I had a vague idea of what he was trying to say. This was the second time Adam had shattered the moment for us. I was surprised to find that I was more than a little angry and a lot irritated.

I was even more surprised when Jude stepped back and his hands dropped to his sides. I shouldn't have been, I guess. But it was such an odd situation. I had felt my emotions swirling around so fast, it was almost like a slap to have them interrupted so suddenly.

I wondered how Jude could step back so easily.

Then I looked up at him again—and I could see that it wasn't easy for him, either. The look in his eyes was fierce, making it more than obvious that it wasn't as easy for him as I had thought.

Slowly, he turned to follow Adam, but he tucked my hand back around his arm, so that we walked together.

As we went, I thought about what had almost happened a few moments ago. . . and the fact that Jude had my hand firmly tucked around his arm.

Inside the caves there were a lot of rules regarding couples. With so little space for everyone—and no sign of being able to spread out anytime soon, the rules about what couples could and could not do were strictly enforced. Even once a couple was bound, there were rules, but they had more freedom to be together in public. However, until they were bound, couples weren't really allowed to be together in public.

Any sign that an unbound couple was getting too close physically, and they would both be punished. So, Jude taking my hand and tucking it around his arm was a very bold and brave gesture. He was sending a message to anyone who happened to see us, and though it still rankled a bit that Adam had broken our moment again, it was exciting for me to realize that Jude did indeed have every intention of pursuing me.

Of course, there was a little voice inside my head that reminded me of the other barriers before us. *He's old enough to be bound, but you're not.* That would be a definite problem. I pushed the thoughts back as we crested the small hill and then struggled and slid down to where the others stood.

We were watching where we were going, so we weren't paying a whole lot of attention to what everyone was staring at, but finally we reached flat ground again and turned to look at everyone standing there.

"OK. What is so important?" I spoke up; knowing my voice was full of venom and not really caring, but no one answered me. No one even looked up.

They were looking at something behind us and when I looked up at Jude, I realized he'd turned and he was looking at it, too. I turned, and when I did, my mouth dropped open in shock and it took a minute for my mind to start forming thoughts again.

We were looking at the remains of a city, a huge city. I had no idea which one it was—and it was really far away, but it was a city, right there for anyone to see. Why had we never heard anything about this? Surely we weren't the only ones to see it. Surely some of the other hunting parties had come this way at some point and seen it.

We just weren't that good, to stumble across something that absolutely no one else had found. It was not a possibility, a bunch of kids finding something on a routine outing that no one else had found in over thirty years.

That was when I started to worry.

I thought back to the last days of my father's life. He had come in from outside duty one night and he'd been almost bouncing out of his boots. I didn't remember ever seeing him so excited. He said he'd found something and it was big. . . huge. . . and very exciting.

He'd told me he had a meeting with the chancellor set up for the next morning. Of course I had asked him what it was all about, but he'd told me he had to prep for his meeting and that he would tell me more about it later.

At the time, I hadn't pushed. I knew he would tell me when he had the time and I knew how important it was for him to be completely ready for his meeting with the chancellor. That was a big deal. He would want to walk into that meeting ready to sound amazing, ready to wow the chancellor, ready to make whatever it was sound like the find of the century.

So I had run off to my room.

He'd had his meeting with the chancellor and he had gone out again two days later and he had never come back.

Well, he'd come back, but he hadn't made it to the compound in time. So, in essence, he'd never come back and the whole thing had gotten swallowed up in my pain and the horrific mourning I went through after that.

I had never thought of it again, until now, anyway. And I had to wonder. . . would my father have been excited about finding a city? Would he have asked for a special meeting with the chancellor over it?

Would he have gone out again on a special trek to check it out?

I thought he would have. I was certain he would have done that. He would have been out there, checking out that city. And it would certainly explain why he'd left so early that morning. He'd left our compartment early enough to be at the gates before they even opened for the morning.

Had he taken a team with him?

If so, what had happened to them? Where had they been when he'd been delayed?

Had the entire team been delayed—or just my father? Had they gone with him to the city or had he ditched them and gone himself only to end up being late getting back to the gates?

If they had gone to the city with him, had something happened while they were there? Had they been forced to leave him? Had they come back without him? And why. . . what could have happened to make them come back without him?

I forced myself to take a deep breath. I knew I was freaking out. My breathing had gotten quicker and harder with each question that rang in my head.

I looked around the group to see if anyone had noticed my craziness.

It didn't seem like it. Every single one of them was staring at the city in the distance. I hoped I was right and they hadn't noticed. If they had missed my freak out, no one would think to ask me why I was panicking over something that should be good. At least they would probably think it was a good thing.

I looked up at the hill when I heard the sound of feet rushing through the snow. It was our instructor and Alan. They were slipping and sliding down the hill, too. Our instructor did not look surprised to see the city, which told me that I was at least partially right. But what really caught my attention was Alan.

Not only did he not look surprised to see the city, he looked angry again—very angry. This, of course, made me wonder.

Was he angry about us finding the city, because he certainly couldn't be angry we found it first since he had clearly already seen it?

So why could he possibly be angry? Was it because we were all so excited about it?

None of those explanations made any sense, though. When I stopped and thought of it, there wasn't much about Alan that did make sense. He was a puzzle. He had always been a puzzle. He didn't really socialize with us, but when we were in class and when we worked out together, he was right there with us all like we were best friends.

He was competitive, but I had always felt like he was doing the same thing I was, holding something back. It was odd and maybe I was wrong about it being a puzzle. Maybe he was just a weird guy. But there was something not right about his face when he saw us having fun in the snow and right now, seeing that we found the city remains. I couldn't put my finger on it. I wasn't even sure I wanted to, but I knew it was not quite right.

And why our instructor looked so panicked; this was also a mystery. He had not looked surprised to see the city when he first slid down the hill, but there hadn't been any trace of fear or panic on his face then.

Now there was. And I could tell he was trying to get it together before he talked to us.

There was only one possible explanation. I was right about the city being a secret. We weren't supposed to find it. He had thought we would stay closer to the complex and hadn't thought to warn us off this area. But he hadn't considered that we were all anxious to get as far from the complex as possible since we had all been attacked or beaten up there recently.

It was an oversight on his part for sure, but it was still a mystery to us why the city would be kept a secret.

It was also a question I didn't want to ask.

If it was something bad enough to make our tough instructor look panicked, especially if there was any chance the city had played a part in my father's disappearance, I wanted nothing to do with it. Now I just had to figure out if that was what he would want from us. And if it was, how could I get everyone else to agree to it, too?

And Jude. . . I thought. *Would he agree to forget we'd ever seen this?*

He had a pretty strong sense of survival, but would he be OK with that big a lie. . . that big a secret? I had no problem with keeping the secret, but I was used to keeping secrets. There were so many my father had shared with me, I'd lost track of just how many there were. I was so used to keeping his secrets, there were actually times I forgot I had secrets. But Jude, would he be able to do it—a secret this huge, this ground-breaking?

I was distracted, thinking about why I was so worried what Jude would do or think or want.

No, we weren't bound. . . and wouldn't be anytime soon, but it was just one more secret. Was that really a surprise here?

Suddenly that voice in my head was back, telling me it was stupid to worry about Jude. He would surely be bound long before I was even old enough.

If he had planned to kiss me, it was only in the interest of curiosity or temporary companionship. He wouldn't want to risk being caught with an underage girl any more than he would want to wait for me to come of age—in which case, it was probably better that we'd been interrupted both times we'd come close to kissing.

If we never kissed, we couldn't form an attachment. And if we never formed an attachment, we couldn't be miserable over the differences in our ages and waiting for one another, and so on.

Aside from all of that, I had enough issues with not being offered an internship and having my father lost outside the gates, I did not need anything else to set me apart from everyone else.

I looked around at the group. They looked like they were all buying the instructor's story about the city and why it needed to stay a secret. I hadn't made up my mind yet, but I had kept so many secrets for so long, I figured one more was really no big deal. That, and I wasn't about to do anything to make myself any more of a target, so I would toe the line.

I felt Jude's hand searching for mine and then gripping it tightly. There was a strange warmth that rushed from my hand where it touched his and went all the way up my arm. I looked down at our entwined hands and then up at his face.

He had a funny look in his eyes and when I started to speak he shook his head a tiny bit. It didn't take more than that to see that he meant whatever he was thinking for my ears—and only mine. So I looked back at the instructor and listened to the rest of what he was saying, while Jude continued to squeeze my hand.

Later that evening, back in the caves, a small group of us sat around a small table in the common area and talked about everything we had seen on our trek outdoors. . . *except* for that secret city.

We talked about all of the intriguing animals we'd encountered, and marveled that we still had not come across another of those crazy tigers. As far and as wide as we had gone from the complex, we were very careful when we talked about how far we'd gone, and no tigers.

I noticed Anna looking guiltily around us to see if anyone had noticed what we were talking about. There was no one else at any of the tables near us. Anna leaned in very close to me and whispered so quietly, I almost couldn't hear her.

"I hate secrets. I'm no good at keeping them. I just know I'm going to mess up and then what will happen?" A shudder went through her when she said that and then she added.

"Not to mention anyone else who happens to hear my slip up." And she looked around again. I reached over to give her hand a squeeze.

"I don't think you have anything to worry about. We're all in on this one. I don't know about everybody else, but I plan to look out for my friends. And I hope you'll help me remember, too." There was no point in telling her that I already knew how to keep a secret.

SIXTEEN

Arizona Caves

Year 45 A.E.

Day 154

It was several days later when everything started to fall apart. We had gone out again, to hunt. This time it was only Jude who was paired with me. We had started pairing up in groups of two, since we now had only ten in the class.

“I really miss Anna.”

“Hmm. . .” was the only response I got from Jude.

Anna had decided she'd had enough training and had gone on to her communications apprenticeship. I never got the chance to ask if it was because of the whole secret city, because she was now in a different area of the complex.

"You have to admit, it's not the same without her. Nothing is the same now."

"What was that, Eve?"

"Oh, nothing really." *Either I mumbled or he is not paying attention to me.* I wanted to be grumpy about it, but I was feeling quite melancholy myself.

We sat there for quite a while just watching the forest around us. It was an odd day. . . eerily silent, still, and clear. It was the kind of day that made me nervous.

I sat there, thinking about all that had gone on over the last few weeks; the hostility of people in the caves, fellow classmates being injured and transferring out of class.

Something about that thought reminded me of Alan. I had made a point of watching him anytime he was around—and the more I watched him—the more confused I was about him.

Nothing he did made any sense.

He was still reclusive whenever we were out of class. But when we were in class he was always with us, pretending we were all buddies. During workouts he was the same way, but the moment we stepped out of class, it was as if he didn't know us.

It was more than a little weird.

Jude had begun to act weird, too.

He held my hand a lot more often—and he was essentially my shadow in the caves. Whenever I went anywhere outside of class, he was right there alongside me.

I would have complained, but it was nice not to have to worry about the attackers that were lurking around all over the complex. With Jude by my side, they'd have to be really stupid to try anything.

It was nice.

And I would have been fine with it, except that I really *couldn't* go anywhere without him.

Somehow he always knew when I was going somewhere. I would go out the hatch and he would be waiting there for me. I kept feeling like there was an axe over my head, like there was something about to happen—something bad.

I really wished I had been wrong.

SEVENTEEN

Arizona Caves

Year 45 A.E.

Day 157

When we came in from hunting, there was a representative from the chancellor's office waiting for us, right inside the gates. She walked over to our instructor and spoke very quietly with him for a few minutes while we stood around, waiting, not knowing if we should stay or leave.

While I was waiting, I decided to check her out. I kept glancing her way, sizing her up. . .

She was ridiculously thin, but not in a way that suggested she was sick, but more like it was on purpose. And her clothes were nothing like I had ever seen before.

The chancellor—the few times I had seen him—was always dressed more like what most of us wore as everyday clothes. His outdoor wear might be a bit fancier than what we had been issued, but nothing like what this woman was wearing.

She was dressed in a tight-fitting jacket over a long skirt, which was also tight-fitting, except for the long slit up the back that I noticed when she turned her back to us.

The material was obviously thick, but not like the everyday clothes those of us in the caves wore.

Isn't she cold? And why would she go around in that kind of outfit in such a cold climate?

The inside of the complex might be heated, but it never really got warm. . . or at least it didn't in the common areas. . . so her clothing seemed completely out of place.

When she turned away from us, turning her body more toward our instructor, I noticed her shoes. They were boots, but they were. . . again, not like any boots I had ever seen before.

The heels were very high and thin and not attached to the rest of the boot like heels usually were. They only touched at the base of the shoe, and then they came down from the bottom like an icicle. The boots themselves looked to be made of some sort of leather and there was a bit of fur around the tops of them, but they looked much too short to be worn with her skirt.

Everything about this woman seemed ridiculous. She was not dressed at all appropriately for the weather—or the rest of the complex for that matter. She was standing here, waiting for us, but she turned her back to the class and spoke only with our instructor . . . and she was very thin—thinner than anyone I could remember seeing.

I was sure I wasn't the only one of us wondering why she was here and what she wanted, but she didn't say a word to us. She simply turned and walked deeper into the complex and our instructor followed. He went a few steps before he seemed to remember we were waiting for instructions. He turned and motioned for us to follow.

They led us through the complex to the area where we dropped off our kills and then they turned toward our classroom, but instead of going to the classroom, they turned down a hall I'd never had an occasion to explore before.

By now, I was curious and I figured everyone else was, too. I looked around at the rest of the class and the expressions all around me sent a shiver up my spine. Here I had been examining the woman's clothing—and I should have been watching her body language and our instructor's expression.

The chill that was working its way up my spine with icy fingers, spread through my chest and I felt the air in my lungs thicken. Then I felt Jude slip his hand into mine and the comforting warmth of his grip helped for a moment before I felt the panic rise up in my throat.

He wouldn't take my hand like this inside without a good reason. This had to mean he was worried for some reason.

So I'm not wrong. . . there is something going on.

My thoughts were swirling around dizzily by then. What exactly should we be worrying about? Had someone slipped and spilled the secret about the city we found? Were we all in trouble because of it? Was that even fair?

Does that even matter?

When I realized how loud my own breath was in the quiet corridor, I forced myself to slow my breathing. Trying to talk some sense into myself, I attempted to come up with things they would need to tell all of us at once—that were not dangerous or came with drastic consequences, but all that I could think of was the young boy in the midst of the group of young people who had been shoved through the gates several weeks ago.

I looked around at the others as we walked. Adam looked bored. Sierra looked cautious, but not frightened or worried. No one looked as panicked as I felt. Some of them looked curious, some just looked worn out—and I could definitely understand that. We were dirty, we were tired, we were still in most of our gear and we were being taken somewhere with no idea of where or why.

Is it possible that they're all just as good as I am at keeping secrets?

The memory of Alan's face that day of the snowball fight popped into my head then. He might be good at hiding his emotions, but I had noticed.

Or did I notice because I saw the anger in his face first? Would I have seen anything off in his expression later if I had not witnessed the transition?

I had no answer, but I watched Alan for some sign of recognition or anger. . . anything that might tell me if he knew what was going on.

But, if he knew anything, there was nothing in his expression to show it.

Finally we reached our destination, or I hoped it was anyway. The outdoor weather gear was beginning to make me sweat and I hoped we would be able to shed it soon or the whole group was going to start to smell.

As soon as that thought came to me, I wondered at the levity in my head. Here we were, possibly about to be in trouble and I was thinking about everyone smelling because we were sweating.

We might be sweating for a whole different reason in a few minutes.

And suddenly I felt cold again; like my insides had turned to ice and even the outdoor weather gear couldn't warm me up. I felt Jude squeeze my hand, but even the warmth of his hand holding mine couldn't touch the ice deep inside me—especially when I saw that our destination was not at all what I had expected.

It was simply a door to another part of the complex. We went through the door, turned the corner and walked into a section of the complex I could never have guessed even existed.

It was. . . plush was the only word I could think to describe it. Instead of being plain gray concrete, the floor here was some sort of patterned rock put together in squares to create a very pleasing pattern.

The walls here were not the plain solid colors we saw everywhere else in the complex, but instead they were covered in what looked like paper and it had a very pretty design etched into it. I looked as closely as I could while keeping up with the group and I noticed the design had a strange shimmer to it.

The lighting was different, too, the lights were recessed into the ceiling and they created a soft look, not the dim, harsh look we had everywhere else. Even the ceilings were different. They were white, not gray and they looked very smooth, not rough and bumpy like the one I looked at every night before I fell asleep.

I realized then that all the white and light colors made the hallway look larger than the ones everywhere else in the complex, even though they were actually the same size. I only knew that because three of us were walking side by side behind the instructor and we could do that in the regular hallways.

Now that I was distracted by the surroundings, I could feel that I was really beginning to warm up.

I had pulled my gloves off when we came inside and I could feel the warmth very strong on my exposed hand. It was nearly as warm on the parts where Jude's hand was not touching as it was where his hand was wrapped around mine and everywhere our hands touched I could feel was beginning to sweat, but I didn't drop his hand.

Her outfit was beginning to make sense to me now. If this was the typical temperature in this part of the complex, her clothes were absolutely perfect for it.

I kept looking around as we walked. We'd followed her around so many corners and past so many rooms with shut doors, I was beginning to lose my bearings and I wasn't sure I could find my way back out if I needed to.

Finally, she stopped walking and gestured for us to move on

through an open doorway nearby. We walked through to find the room beyond was just as nice as the hall we had just came from, maybe even a bit fancier. There was a large, round table in the middle of the room and she was motioning for us to have a seat.

After a moment, when we all stood there looking at her, she seemed to realize we were all still bundled up and we couldn't possibly sit in these chairs with everything we were wearing. She shook her head a little and a slightly embarrassed smile crossed her face.

"Feel free to shed your outerwear. I apologize for not suggesting it sooner, but we felt it was important to move quickly." As soon as she had told us to, we had started shedding our packs and coats and the heavy outer boots we wore outside. We pulled scarves from around our necks and tucked gloves into pockets.

Not seeing anywhere else to put them, we lined everything up along one wall of the room, trying to keep the piles as neat as possible in our hurry to shed as much as we could—as quickly as we could.

Then, one by one, we made our way to the large table and found a seat.

Jude, of course, sat in the chair to the right of me. I was actually a bit torn about how to feel about that, but I used it as a distraction. I needed to calm down and this was as good a reason as any to distract myself.

I wanted to be grateful that he was sticking close to me, like in the hallways around the complex and whenever we went outside. But on the other hand, there was a small part of me that found it a little annoying that he was always there—like a shadow or a guard or. . . something.

Did he really think, especially after that night I'd been attacked, that I couldn't take care of myself?

I remembered that recently I had told myself how lucky I was that Jude was acting as a shadow—and that I was thankful for his protection. Now, I was feeling stifled.

This is ridiculous! I need to choose a side and stick with it!

I shook those thoughts away. It didn't seem to matter one way or the other. He'd decided he was going to shadow me and that was that. So I had better just get used to it. Not to mention, this was hardly the time to think about it.

Fortunately, I was distracted then by the door opening and the chancellor walking in. I had only ever seen the chancellor when he addressed the entire complex and even then it was from a distance. But here he was, right in front of me—and obviously he was here to talk to us.

He walked to the end of the table and stood there, talking quietly with the woman who had brought us here. After a minute or two, he turned to face us, with a sad smile on his face.

"I regret to have to tell you this, but it has to be done, and we wanted you to hear about it firsthand and not from the gossips." He paused for a moment and it looked like he was trying to make himself say something he really didn't want to say.

"Your classmate, Anna, was found dead this morning." There were gasps all around the table.

Lily started crying.

He smiled sympathetically at her, and then continued speaking. "We are still not certain of what happened, but we have determined that she was on her way to her communications quarters after she finished her evening session when she was attacked. She was not expected by anyone until this morning, so no one even realized she was missing until it was already too late."

He stopped speaking then – and I thought about what he had said. . . and what he had not. If she had stayed with our class, we would probably have been walking to and from things together still and she would have had at least some protection when the attackers came at her.

Or—they might not even have come at her. The groups we had stayed in lately tended to discourage them.

She quit the class to protect herself and then she died anyway.

"I hope it will be a small comfort to know that we will not stop until we discover who is responsible for this heinous crime."

I was shocked at his words.

Comfort? Is he serious?

How could anything be a comfort to us right now! And I realized I was crying, too. The tears were rolling fast and hot down my cheeks. I reached up to dash the tears away and forgot to put my hand back in my lap and Jude reached over just as I dropped it and wrapped his fingers around mine and gave my hand a light squeeze.

And that was too much for me. I turned my chair and threw myself into his arms.

He wrapped both arms around me and rubbed one hand up and down my back slowly as I sobbed into his chest. I didn't even care what anyone else thought of my behavior. I just knew I needed comfort and he was the only one I wanted to give it.

I felt so many things drain out of me with those tears. I felt all the anger I had been holding in at my father walking away from the city flow out with them. I felt anger I hadn't known I felt for my mother and my grandparents rush away.

I felt the hardness that had built up around my heart over the past few years—begin to soften. I had never let myself get too close to people and now I could see why. I had been too frightened of losing them the way I'd lost my father. Yet it hadn't done a bit of good, because here I was grieving anyway.

With that realization, came the knowledge that Anna had been the closest I'd had to a friend—and my heart felt like it was breaking open for her.

I was letting her into my heart only now, after she was gone. I thought about all the other students in the room who might be feeling the same pain I was dealing with right now and I finally started to feel myself calm down a little. I started to notice the soft strokes of Jude's hand on my back. I felt his other arm tight around me as he held me close to him.

As my own sobs calmed, I became more aware of the other sobs in the room. Lily was sobbing quietly, but the sound of her soft sobs was heart breaking. It almost undid me again.

To distract myself, I looked around the table at the rest of the class.

Jake was trying to comfort Lily, but he didn't seem to be having much luck. Jordan and Sophia were whispering between themselves, taking advantage of the chance to sit close and not have anyone give them a hard time about it.

They were old enough, but they weren't bound yet, so the public affection was off-limits and we all knew it. We all knew they found quiet places to be together when we were out hunting or exploring, but so far, no one had called them on it or reported them.

Adam and Sierra looked bored. I thought that was a bit odd since they had both grown up with Anna and had lived in the same section, but there was not really anything I could say.

As I looked away, I noticed that Malcolm looked like he was fighting with an emotion that resembled something more like anger than sadness.

Had he been close to Anna? I thought back to our times outside, but I couldn't remember them being close.

Maybe he was just a protective person.

That was when I realized Alan was missing. He was nowhere to be found. Just as I started to say something, Jude squeezed my hand. Then he whispered to me, his voice barely audible even though his mouth was right next to my ear.

"He slipped out when everyone began to break down. I do not think anyone has noticed but you and me." The look he gave me said everything; I needed to keep it to myself. I opened my mouth to ask Jude to tell me more about his own suspicions, but then I thought back to the look on Alan's face when we had found the city.

There was more going on there than I knew. . . *Maybe more than any of us know.* And the most horrific thought occurred to me at that moment.

Did Alan have something to do with Anna's death?

I actually slapped my hand over my mouth at the very thought that it could be possible. Even though I hadn't said anything, I didn't really want to think it and I was horrified it had come out of me, even just in a thought—and I snuggled back against Jude's chest, wishing that I could be anywhere else right now.

I was surprised to discover that I was just as exhausted as I was angry. What right did Alan or anyone else have to make this time about them?

Why would anyone be so callous to pick such a time to go off and do something stupid? Really! They couldn't wait a few minutes...

Jude's hand rubbed gently across my back again and I wrapped a hand around part of his shirt. No matter what was going on with Alan or Adam or Sierra, Jude's arms were comforting. I did not want to be anywhere else right this moment.

However, life being what it was, I did not get my wish. The woman who had brought us into the room cleared her throat and then started speaking again. Her voice was soft and sweet, but her words still irritated me.

"The chancellor wants to make sure you understand that we will do everything in our power to bring these criminals to justice. Also, we intend to provide security—for those of you who would like to take advantage of it." She stopped for a moment before going on. When she continued; her voice was different—more business-like.

“We do not wish to rush you off, but we feel it would benefit you all if you were to move somewhere a bit more comfortable.” She was perfectly nice about it, but the meaning was clear, at least to me.

They wanted their fancy conference room back and they wanted us dirty civilians out of their nice clean area.

EIGHTEEN

Arizona Caves

Year 45 A.E.

Same Day

Back in our section of the complex, we headed for the classroom and our prep area.

We stowed our gear, changed back into our indoor wear. Most of us gathered in the common room to talk about what had happened that day.

Sophia and Jordan were conspicuously absent, and I hadn't seen Alan since Jude pointed out that he was gone, but everyone else was there—even Adam and Sierra.

"So, what are we going to do about this?" Adam's gruff voice belied the fact that he felt more over Anna's death than he had let on earlier.

“Yeah, I'm with Adam. We can't just let these idiots hunt us down one at a time.” Jake spoke next, standing as he did so, fists clenched at his sides.

“If we work together, we can take them. No problem.” Sierra may have spoken quietly, but her voice was anything but soft. They might not be upset over Anna's death, but they were all for us hunting for these attackers on our own.

“We're all trained in hand-to-hand combat now and we've done so much working out, I know we could handle these guys, whoever they are.”

I was a little shocked. I had never figured Sierra for being so blood thirsty, but there were clearly more than a few things I'd missed about my classmates.

“No, that's not what I meant.” Adam was shaking his head as he objected. “We can't just form an attack group of our own, Sierra. The guards would never stand for it. We would end up being just as guilty as they are when it comes time for punishment.”

I was nodding my head before he finished.

Adam would know. He had already been accepted into the Guard program. He just had to finish out this class and then he could start his training there.

"I'm with Jake and Sierra. We can't just let these guys pick us off one by one."

I felt my mouth drop open. I never expected to hear those words from Malcolm. He was always so quiet and reserved. I really didn't know my classmates like I thought I did.

"Now listen. . ." he raised his voice a little to be heard over the sudden rush of voices from the whole group. "Just listen to me and then argue." He looked around at us as he said it, and in an unspoken agreement, we all quieted so he could finish.

"What I mean is, these attackers are organized and sneaky. They're vicious and they're methodical. If we stick together in groups, they'll just wait and watch until one of us drops our guard and goes out alone. If we take the extra protection—same thing. They'll wait until the protection thinks the danger has passed and then they'll strike. They've already done it."

He looked around at us again before going on.

"Think about it. We started grouping whenever we went anywhere and the attacks slowed down or stopped. Then Anna decided to leave the class, thinking it would make her safe—and then, when she wasn't with us anymore, she was going somewhere alone, and that's when they got her." He slapped the table in front of us for emphasis.

"He's got a point."

I looked over at Lily. For some reason, I wasn't surprised that she agreed with Sierra and Jake and Malcolm.

She had a reputation in the group for being impulsive and it had gotten her into trouble more than once.

And then I heard the voice of reason from beside me and I turned to him, grateful he was so sensible. But I could not have been more surprised by what he said.

"Malcolm is correct. These criminals do not follow the rules we live by. They feel as if they can do whatever they want. We cannot allow them to get away with it, and we cannot continue thinking that we can ignore them to make them stop what they are doing." His voice was so quiet, just like I had heard it so many times and I felt myself wanting to agree with him.

But then I remembered my father. I remembered wanting to go after the chancellor, the other guards and the gate keepers. For weeks, I had plotted and planned and then my Grandad had taken me aside and explained to me the major flaw in my plans.

He had told me he understood my feelings, because he had them, too. He hated the rule that had killed his son. He hated the guards who had continued closing the gate, when they could clearly see how close my father had been to making it. He hated the chancellor, who had made the law that said the gates closed at a certain time each night and they would not be held open for anyone.

But then he told me to think about the other children who would lose a father if either of us were to carry out a plan that caused one of those men harm.

He told me to think of my mother and my grandmother.

If either of us did harm to one of the guards or the gatekeepers —or especially the chancellor—we would be treated like criminals and our fate would be the same as my father's.

Only we would not have just been late getting to the gate, we would be executed. Not only would they lose us, they would have to live with everyone treating them differently forever after, because they were the mother and the grandmother of a criminal, the daughter and wife of a criminal.

I had never figured out if he put himself in the scenario with me to make it more real to me or to make it clear that I would not act alone and any action I took, he would, too—so any punishment I received, he would receive.

Whatever it was about the explanation, it worked and I began in that moment to examine my behaviors, all of them looking at how they would affect everyone around me and not just myself.

It made a tremendous difference in how I did things after that. And of course, it was after that conversation and my subsequent change in behavior, that my Grandfather began teaching me about self-defense and sharing his hunting techniques. He saw that I was able to see things more logically. Something about that made him decide to teach me those things.

He was one of the few people in the caves who did things occasionally that didn't make sense at the time. But later, when looking back, they made perfect sense. And I was glad he had seen whatever it was in me that made him teach me self-defense.

It had probably saved my life. I wished again that I had somehow been able to save Anna. But I had not. Now I had to find a way to honor her memory by keeping my fellow students from doing something that could get them all killed.

I didn't know I would never get the chance.

I opened my mouth to speak, but the first word never had the chance to even form.

From across the room, we heard screaming. It was not like any scream I had ever heard before. It was like a trapped animal that was slowly being ripped to pieces.

Every word, every conversation in the common area came to a halt as we all looked toward where the scream was coming from. A moment later, we saw Sophia running out of one of the darker hallways.

She was bleeding—a lot. We could see that, even from across the enormous room. Her clothes were ripped and hanging in shreds. I couldn't even begin to think what could have happened to her.

We rushed over toward her. Because she was running and still screaming; clearly hysterical, it took all of us to catch her. She fought us as she thrashed around like she was still being attacked.

I don't know how he managed to get close enough, but Jude put a hand on either side of her face and forced her to look at him as he spoke slowly and calmly, telling her that she was safe now—and finally she began to calm down.

When she stopped, it was like all of the fight had gone out of her. She collapsed and would have hit the floor had we not all been right there to catch her.

Adam was the closest to her. He lifted her up into his arms gently and headed for the infirmary. We followed, looking at each other as we went.

Before Adam had moved ten feet, Sophia started fighting again and she almost fell out of his arms as she struggled to try and get down. She was babbling almost incoherently, but Jude picked up enough on what she was saying, somehow, and told her we would go.

He grabbed my hand and said something quickly to Malcolm, then turned to the others—Adam and Sierra, Jake and Lily—and told them to get Sophia to the infirmary.

Adam hesitated. "Are you sure you got it?" He looked at us as he spoke and Jude answered.

"I don't expect them to still be there. They would not stay, not with all the screaming she did. It attracted too much attention. Honestly, I am more worried about her. If she got a good look. . ." He let his words trail off.

Adam nodded and headed off toward the infirmary.

Jude still had my hand in his as he headed for the hall Sophia had just come from. He stopped though, just before we headed down the hall and turned to look at me.

"I do not think I really gave this enough thought. Would you prefer to stay here? This could be a very bad idea. . ."

He left the end of the sentence hanging, almost like it was a question. I couldn't tell if he was telling me that he hadn't thought about how dangerous it could be or if he was thinking I was better off not seeing the results of the attack.

Either way, I knew there was no way I was sitting here in the square while he went off into that dark hallway. If there was a group of attackers there, I could defend myself well-enough. And if Jordan was down that hall somewhere, he probably needed our help. So I shook my head and squeezed his hand.

"I'm good. Let's go. Hurry." And I started off toward the hallway. He really had no choice but to follow, or pull his hand free, so he followed me.

Malcolm was right behind us and I felt immensely better with Jude at my side and Malcolm at my back. I remembered from our times paired together hunting that he had exceptionally good hearing. That would come in handy if someone was lying in wait to attack whoever came down this hall.

We did not find any attackers, though.

We probably went twenty feet when Malcolm rushed ahead. Jude and I moved faster to catch up to him, but he was obviously faster than we realized. Or else, something had given him a sudden burst of speed.

Maybe he heard the attackers and he wanted to surprise them.

That thought made me move a bit faster, too. I did not want him to get there ahead of us and be alone with those criminals.

Fortunately, Jude sped up with me. I held his hand tightly as we ran.

I didn't want to be separated from him, especially now. I told myself I would think about what that meant later, because now was not the time. We turned another corner and saw why Malcolm had sped up, but we saw that it was too late to do anything about it.

Jordan lay there in a rapidly spreading puddle of blood. There was hardly a part of him that wasn't covered in cuts or scrapes or bruises, many of them on top of each other.

It was not a pretty sight and I was glad we weren't finding Sophia there beside him, in the same shape. I turned to look at Jude and I was surprised to realize there were tears in my eyes.

"Is there anything. . ." I couldn't even finish the sentence, but he knew what I meant.

Jude was shaking his head before I even said the words. I looked at him and then down at Malcolm, who was down on one knee and leaning in close to Jordan. He was shaking his head and then he told us what Jude had already figured out, his voice barely a whisper.

"He's gone now." Malcolm stayed there on his knees for another minute before standing. Then we all stood there for several minutes in silence.

Finally he spoke again.

"I heard him. That's why I rushed ahead. He was alive when I got here. I could barely hear him, but he was asking about

Sophia." He paused a second and I heard a strange noise, like a strangled cough, before he went on.

"I told him she was all right. Do you think that was a good thing to do? I mean, we don't really know if she will be. . ." He trailed off, looking at us with a hint of desperation in his eyes.

I looked over at Jude, but I couldn't think why it would be a bad thing to reassure a dying man. He was just standing there, looking down at Jordan, so I said the only thing I could think of.

"It was the right thing to do. When we saw her, she was alive and Adam took her to get help. I'm sure she'll be fine." I put my hand on Malcolm's shoulder and squeezed. Then I turned at the sound of running feet.

"Should we. . .?"

But I was too late. Suddenly we were surrounded by guards and security personnel. They had brought light with them and I could see Jordan's body much better than I could ever have wanted to.

I cringed at the sight and turned into Jude's arms.

I didn't even want to think about how painful his last few minutes had been. And his only concern had been for Sophia.

I looked to the nearest guard, but before I could even say a word, we were all slammed up against the nearest wall, arms twisted behind our backs and the guards were shouting in our ears.

Even though I knew I had done nothing, I knew better than to fight the guards, so I cooperated as well as I could.

I felt a sharp sting on my temple, so I must have missed a direction. I tried to listen better, but everything in my head was suddenly fuzzy and my vision had a strange wiggle at the edges.

NINETEEN

Arizona Caves

Year 45 A.E.

Day 158

I woke to Jude's furious whispering.

"Eve, you have to wake up, now! Really, come out of it. I do not know how long we have until they return." He sounded really upset about something, but I couldn't seem to get my eyes to open, no matter how much I might want them to. Finally I decided to give my voice a try.

"Whass goinon?" And I knew that wasn't right. What was wrong with me? Those were the words I wanted to say, but why did they sound so funny?

"They may come back any second now. I know not what is going on, but someone must have covered for us. You have a concussion and have been mumbling about that blasted city. You cannot keep doing that! You will get yourself in even worse trouble."

His voice was a furious whisper and his lips had to be right by my ear, because it felt like there was a hot wind blowing past it. I tried to make sense of his words. They were all running together in my head and rolling around, getting mixed up. It felt like I lay there for an eternity, trying to make sense of it all before his last three words finally made sense.

My eyes popped open and I finally felt awake. I was feeling groggy and dizzy, and there was still a wavy blur around my vision, but it started to clear as I sat up and looked around.

Jude was sitting on the edge of the bed next to me and his face was covered in some pretty nasty cuts - some of which were crusted over and bruises that were already turning a nasty shade of green.

How long had I been out? Why hadn't anyone woken me up before now?

There was also a long bandage that disappeared under his shirt. I could only see a little of it, but I had a feeling that there was a lot more of it under his shirt.

Malcolm was standing between the two beds and his face was

equally bruised and both his lips were split. One of his fingers was in a splint and he seemed to be standing very stiff. It looked like he was breathing kind of shallow.

I could see bandages in several places and one of them looked like it needed to be changed because I could see a large, dark stain running down the middle of it.

What had happened to them? What had happened to me?

Jude said I had a concussion.

How did I get a concussion?

Before any more questions could form in my mind, it all came rushing back; Sophia running out of the hallway, Adam scooping her up and heading to the infirmary with her, Jude and me and Malcolm heading off to see if there was anything we could do for Jordan. The guards showing up and obviously thinking we had something to do with what happened to Jordan, then the searing pain in my temple and everything going black.

I pressed my fingers to my temples as the images rushed into my head and noticed a pain in the fingers touching my right temple. I pulled my hand away to look at my fingers. They were taped up, but they looked terrible and they felt even worse.

"What do you mean, 'even more trouble'?" I wanted to say more, but the urge to vomit was so strong and so sudden, I was afraid to open my mouth again.

I looked at him and waited for an answer, hoping he would figure out why I wasn't speaking without my actually having to open my mouth. At the same time, I hoped desperately that I would not vomit.

I hated to be sick.

"I do not know. I only know we are not in the regular infirmary and that seems like trouble to me. I cannot imagine why they would have us here if we were not still in trouble—unless they are afraid to move you."

He looked around him again and then leaned back in close to me.

"No one has told us anything. Someone came just after that guard hit you and we were brought here instead of to a cell. They were whispering so I did not catch much of it. Since I was shoved up against a wall at the time, I did not get a look at who it was who was doing the ordering. I only know they were more gentle with us after that."

Before he could say anything else, the door at the end of the room opened and a group of people came in. I looked, but my vision was still quite a bit blurry, so I couldn't see much more than that it was a crowd.

They were all talking at once as they came toward us and then suddenly, everyone stopped talking—all at once.

They were close enough now that I could make some of them out. I could see the woman we had seen earlier toward the front of the group and several other people who were dressed exactly like her. I couldn't help thinking that they must be cold in this part of the complex.

Or maybe that was why they were huddled so close together; they were sharing body heat as they moved.

I tried to figure out why my thoughts were still so fuzzy. Then I remembered Jude saying I had a concussion. That must be why I couldn't seem to concentrate on anything for very long. And it would explain why nothing made sense in my head.

But I knew I needed to concentrate.

These people were coming down here to do something and they all looked very serious. We could be in a lot of trouble and I did not want to say anything to make it worse. I didn't dare shake my head, but I did everything else I could think of to try and clear it.

Two hours later, I was walking down the hall between Jude, who was hobbling slowly on my right and Malcolm who was walking just as carefully on my left. I still couldn't believe what had happened in that room.

Imagine the chancellor himself coming to apologize to us about the guard's behavior when they had arrested us.

It almost made me want to stop thinking badly of him. . . almost.

He had explained that the guards were under strict orders to capture the group who was responsible for all the attacks recently, but they were only supposed to react so violently in the case of resistance.

No one had actually said the guards were in any trouble, but it had been implied—or so I thought. He had also told us there really was no excuse for what had happened to us, but that the guards must have thought we were the attackers and had gotten a bit carried away in their zeal to capture the ones they were sure had now killed two young people in as many days.

That had confirmed what we already knew, not officially, of course, but Malcolm had said as much.

Jordan was gone, too.

Jude asked about Sophia and we were told she was doing well, so far as her injuries were concerned, but her mental state was fragile and she was heavily sedated because of it.

That made me wonder who had actually identified us, but in truth, it could have been anyone in the class or even someone who had watched us rush off into the corridor *after* Sophia had come running out, already covered in blood and screaming her head off.

When the chancellor had finished, asking if we wished to stay where we were. . . or move to the other infirmary, we had wasted no time in high-tailing it out of there.

The nurses and doctors hadn't really wanted to let us go, but the chancellor had pointed out that we were all able to stand and move on our own and that we had clearly been through enough already. So, they'd really had no choice but to release us.

I had taken time to visit the bathroom where I had seen the extent of the injuries on my face. I got a pretty good idea of how bad the rest of them were, too, but I hadn't wanted to spend a lot more time in this place, so it was a quick look.

My right eye was all sorts of colors already—and looked like it was already swelling. There was a bandage over my left eye; I thought I could see a little blood seeping along the inside of it. That must be where the guard had hit me and I found myself wondering what he'd hit me with. It had left some pretty nasty damage behind.

There were bruises on both my cheeks and in several places along my collarbone. I had a split lip, too.

I had cuts and scrapes on my hands, probably from where I had tried to catch myself as I went down and I could feel bruises in other places, but I didn't take the time to find them all. I just wanted to get out of there.

After I finished in the bathroom, I went out to find that Malcolm had fresh bandages and Jude was holding onto a pair of crutches. They both looked ready to go, but the nurse made me wait until she replaced my bandage, too.

I couldn't tell if she did it on purpose or not, but when she pulled it off, she was moving extremely slowly and it stuck to the cut, so the pain was drawn out and I wanted so desperately to scream, but I knew that would be a bad idea.

There was little doubt that any hint that we couldn't handle our injuries would mean we would not be going anywhere.

I started to feel a tiny bit better when I looked over at Malcolm and saw his look that said he had been through the same thing. And then I looked at Jude and his look actually gave me the strength to keep my mouth shut.

He looked sorry for what they were doing to me, but he also looked like he was very proud of me and that made me feel so great, I almost didn't even feel the pain anymore.

Almost.

Now we were making our way slowly back to the main section, looking for the rest of the class as we went, and hoping we could find out a bit more about Sophia.

I was moving as slowly as possible due to the nausea that continued to threaten me, and the ache in every single one of my limbs.

I had a feeling Malcolm was moving as slowly as me because of his cracked ribs, but Jude didn't seem to be struggling at all, so I felt like he must be slowing down on purpose.

And this one time. . . I really didn't mind. It was smart for us to stick together, especially now. I knew that Malcolm and I would be easy targets for anyone right now. At least Jude had crutches he could use as weapons if he had to.

So I concentrated on moving slowly and trying to keep my head from moving any more than possible.

After what seemed like forever, we reached the main square and looked around for the rest of the class. They were nowhere to be found, but we were surprised to see that there were hardly any other people there. I turned to the guys.

"What time is it? How long were we there?"

We all knew it was tricky to tell the time around here. The halls were usually dark. The main areas were usually about half-lit and there were only a few clocks scattered around the complex. Mostly they were in offices and important places.

Most of us had personal timepieces, but all of our personal belongings had been taken when we were arrested. They'd returned everything, but we hadn't taken the time to pull it all out of the bags they'd handed us just before they released us. We were determined to get out of there as fast as we could.

Fortunately, I remembered the bags.

"Our stuff is in these bags, right?" I held up my bag and Jude's. I'd taken his when we left because I knew it would be harder for him to maneuver the crutches if he had to carry the bag, too.

Jude nodded and we made our way over to the nearest table and I emptied Jude's bag and then mine while Malcolm slid everything out of his own bag. Our stuff mingled together on the tabletop and made a big mess.

I picked through the pile until I came up with my digital. The face had a new crack running along the edge and I had a pretty good idea where it had come from, but I wasn't about to push anything about getting it fixed.

My vision was still a little blurry so it took me a few seconds to figure out what it read and I was surprised to see that it was 2

A.M. There was something about that time that bothered me, but my head was still so fuzzy and the thoughts would not come clear.

And then it came clear. . . a little too clear.

The memories of that early morning execution came rushing back and set off my nausea all over again in the process.

It was 2 A.M.

I could hardly believe the odds. I looked up at Jude and Malcolm. They both had their digitals back on by now and were sorting through the rest of the scattered belongings on the table. Neither showed even a little bit of recognition about that morning or the irony that it was now 2 A.M.

The same time this most recent mess really started. . .

Maybe there was no connection.

Maybe it was just a coincidence.

Maybe it was only me who held onto the images of those children, bruised, bleeding and with no coats or shoes and the total absence of an adult taking responsibility for them.

That memory got me thinking. The storms that had started that very morning had gone on for several weeks and everyone had been stuck indoors for the duration.

For a long time, people had gone around looking at each other like they were criminals. I had actually joined the class in an attempt to alleviate some of the boredom and get away from all the angry people.

But no adults had ever come forward. No adults had ever been captured or executed, unless for some reason it had been kept quiet.

Why?

There was no good reason that I could think of, but it was obvious there was a lot that went on in the caves that I didn't know about, a lot that very few people actually knew anything about. I found myself wondering who besides the chancellor knew everything about what went on in the caves.

Was there even one other person?

I didn't have any more time to wonder because Adam's voice suddenly interrupted my thoughts. And I cringed because his voice was loud and a little too exuberant for me.

"Whoa. So they were still there, huh. How many of them were there?" And then his voice turned serious.

"How bad was Jordan when you got there?" While he waited for us to answer, we looked at each other, trying to decide which question to answer first, how to break the rough news to him and just how much to tell him about the rest.

Fortunately Jude decided to be the one to break the bad news, for which I was incredibly grateful.

"It is more complicated than that, but. . ." He paused for just a second before going on. "I thought for certain someone would have told you all."

That was all Adam needed to understand what Jude was saying.

"Oh, man. Jordan didn't make it then? That's gonna just kill Sophia. She's not doin real good, guys. I just left the infirmary. The nurse kicked me out. Said I'm no good to my friend if I'm dead on my feet." It took a second, but he got what he'd just said. "Sorry. Didn't mean to. . ." And he let his words trail off.

We sat there for what felt like a long time, but when I looked at my digital again, it was only about twenty minutes. Finally Adam spoke up again.

"What did you mean when you said the rest of it was complicated?" He looked at Jude and Jude looked at me and then Malcolm. We both nodded to him and he launched into the explanation.

"Jordan was still alive when we reached him. His last words were to ask if Sophia was OK."

"We should tell her that whenever she's up to hearing it." Malcolm interrupted.

Jude nodded, and went on. “Yes, I think she would like to know that. But maybe we should skip over how he looked.”

We all agreed and he kept going. “Whoever attacked Jordan and Sophia was gone when we arrived.”

This time Adam interrupted. “What happened to you three, then?”

“The guards came and—” Jude paused for a moment. He looked like he was trying to figure out exactly how to say it, but I knew he was trying to decide if he should tell Adam the excuse we had been given, or what we thought had happened.

Right then I knew there was something Jude knew—like what I knew—that he shouldn't.

He had some sort of secret that was just like the ones I had, and he knew that there was a lot more going on around here than most people realized. It made me really glad he was the one doing the talking. He certainly seemed to know the right thing to say and even how to say it.

“Let me just say that the guards were a bit over-zealous, when they thought they had captured the ones responsible for two deaths.”

Adam was gaping now, he looked completely shocked. It made me really glad Jude had kept it to what he'd said and that he'd kept it short and sweet. I didn't think Adam could have handled much more than that. He was just sitting there, looking from Jude to me to Malcolm and back again.

“Hey, we'll live. At least they figured out what was going on before it went too far. They took us down to the infirmary and the chancellor himself came down to apologize.” Malcolm said with a slightly crooked grin.

I realized his split lips weren't letting him smile right and I wanted so badly in that moment to say something else, anything else, about what had really happened, but I knew Jude and Malcolm had the right idea.

Adam was in line for the guard training program. It would not be a good idea to give him the wrong impression of them now. There was no telling what he would do with it. And the last thing any of us needed was more trouble.

So I sat there, not saying anything, letting Jude and Malcom do the talking. It was just easier.

I felt a little better when I felt Jude squeeze my hand under the table. And I was amazed to discover how happy I was about it.

Only a few hours ago I had been so irritated with him, I'd purposely kept my hand where he couldn't possible reach it.

Of course, then I had collapsed into his arms when we were told about Anna and I'd cried like a baby. Then I'd held his hand all the way back into this section of the compound and later, when we went down the hallway to see what we could do for Jordan.

I hadn't held his hand since waking up in the other infirmary, but he'd been using crutches, so it wasn't easy to imagine him finding a way to hold my hand while he maneuvered crutches, too. But he was holding my hand now and I felt so much better because he was.

It made all the rest of it seem a little less frightening; the secrets, that crazy city, all the things we all suspected about how things really worked around here. Somehow they seemed a little less threatening and that felt like a miracle.

I didn't remember feeling so safe with anyone since before my father had died and I liked it. And suddenly I didn't care any more about whether or not we could have a real relationship or not.

The differences in our ages didn't matter to me at all any more. Not much of anything mattered to me right this minute. I was just concentrating on the feel of his hand in mine. Between what happened to Anna and Jordan and what happened to Sophia, it felt vitally important to enjoy this moment and stretch it out as long as we could.

But it wasn't meant to be.

Only a few minutes had passed when someone came by and reminded us that we were out past curfew. We had really only stopped to rest on the way to our sections. We knew we couldn't sit here all night and we needed to get some rest, too.

We all stood and headed slowly to the living sections. As luck would have it, we got to my section first and Jude insisted they walk me right to the hatch.

I was hesitant to go in—and I worried about the three of them, as well. What would they do when there was only one of them left?

"Don't worry." Malcolm told me. "Jude and I are in the same hallway." I nodded and turned to punch in the code at my hatch.

My grandmother was standing there when the hatch opened and she looked like she'd been crying.

I tried not to feel guilty. It wasn't like I could help what had happened to me that evening, but I knew what she must have been thinking, and I did feel guilty. I made my goodbye quick.

"Night, guys. Take it nice and slow, Jude." He stayed there for another few seconds, just looking at me before he nodded and turned away to follow Malcolm and Adam down the corridor.

I turned back to my grandmother and I was immediately swallowed up in her embrace. I cringed, but didn't pull away—even when she squeezed and the nausea rose in my throat. I just clamped my lips shut and reminded myself of how worried she must have been all this time.

I could tell by the tracks down her cheeks that she had been crying for some time now. She was still crying a little, but she didn't look angry, so I felt a little better. She could probably tell what shape I was in—and she knew about the other attacks so she'd probably put two and two together and come up with a rough idea of what had happened.

I was in the same place I'd been a while ago.

How much should I tell her? And how was I supposed to figure out how to make what had happened sound less frightening and dangerous than it had been?

Would she be angry with me for going down that hallway?

Would she be able to see how much more dangerous it would have been for me to stay behind—all alone?

I was saved from having to explain, when the hatch opened behind me, and my Grandfather came through the hatch.

"She got in OK this afternoon. Apparently her class was rushed off to some meeting as soon as they came in and. . ." He stopped—right in the middle of his sentence, when he saw me—and then he was rushing over and hugging me.

They were both pushing on tender spots. My head felt like it was about to explode, but I wasn't about to say anything to them about any of that. They had been sitting here all evening, probably thinking I was dead.

A little more pain on my part was nothing compared to the worry and anguish they had been through. I remembered how bad it had been with my father and I imagined this had been close to the same.

“Oh we've been so worried. We had no idea what happened to you. Kids keep getting attacked in the halls and then we heard about that girl who dropped your class and we didn't know if it was related or not, but we couldn't find anyone who knew anything. We've been worried sick.”

“Where's Mom?” It had occurred to me earlier, but I figured I knew the answer so I'd waited until I couldn't stand being squeezed any more to ask.

They looked at each other over my head before they answered.

“She's taken a sedative and she's sleeping. I don't know if we can wake her up, but I think we should try.” Grandmother said and I agreed.

“I'm willing to try. I hate that she went to sleep not knowing what happened to me.” And then my appearance occurred to me. “Do you think I'll scare her, looking like this?”

Grandad was the one who answered. “I really don't think she'll care much about what you look like. Well, she'll be worried about you, but it can't be helped. I do think it'll be worse if we don't at least try.”

Grandmother was beside him, nodding her head as she dabbed at her tears. So I headed down the little hall to her room.

It usually only took me a few seconds to make the trip to her room, but tonight, hampered by my injuries and my grandparents clinging tightly to me, it took a lot longer. And, all the way down the hall, I was reminded of the night my father had not made it to the gates in time.

I remembered being dragged to the infirmary, not the one I had been in tonight and not the one I'd been in when Jude and I had collided.

They had them in several sections of the complex and Grandad had taken me to the closest one to him that night.

I didn't really remember much about that infirmary, except that it was a lot smaller than the main one I had been in many times over the years and even a bit smaller than the one close to the workout areas.

If I had to guess, it was probably just for guards and people who were hurt outside, but not seriously injured.

They had given me a strong sedative and I'd been unconscious pretty fast, which was why I remembered so little. But later, I had woken up in my own bed to the sound of my mother crying. It was a terrible, heart-wrenching sound. I remembered how it tore through me and made me feel much worse, like the world had come to an end.

So many of those memories were still fresh in my mind. I had made a point over the years to keep them that way, because it was the only way I could think to keep my father with me.

Those memories and the ones just before that time were the clearest, and I was glad of it.

It also helped remind me that I knew there was something going on around here that was not quite right.

And even though it wasn't my fault. . . even though everything that had happened tonight had been completely beyond my control. . . even though I could not have done anything differently, even if I had wanted to, I felt terrible about this whole mess.

My mother had worried for hours, not knowing what was going on with me, not knowing if I was alive or dead. No one had come to tell her I was in the infirmary or that I had been in the custody of security. No one had come to tell my family where I was or what had happened to me. I couldn't figure out why or what to do about it.

Her hatch was open, so we went in without bothering to knock. Right away I could hear soft sobs, not the deep, even breathing I had expected, and I knew it meant that she was awake. What had happened to the sedative?

Had they given her something that had already worn off?

Why would they do that? With that thought, anger spread through me. She had either been up to the infirmary to get a sedative or someone had come down here to give it to her. Why had no one been able to let her know what was going on with her daughter? Were they really so incompetent. . . or had they done it on purpose?

Approaching her bed, I took several deep breaths. I still had no idea what to tell her about today and all that had happened.

My first instinct was to do whatever I could to protect her. I didn't want to tell her too much, but I had to give her some details.

Maybe it would be enough to tell her what Jude had told Adam.

I could even give her a few more details without telling her too much, or going into my own suspicions.

I would never know if she heard us or had noticed the light from the hallway.

One second I was moving through the open doorway and the next, I was wrapped tightly in her arms and the two of us were rocking back and forth and crying, our tears and sobs so mixed together, they sounded like one person.

After what felt like a very long time, Mom pulled back and looked at my face. Then she touched a finger very carefully beside every single bruise and cut on my face. With each one she got more and more quiet until the tears had completely stopped and she nodded. Then she got to her feet and gently pulled me up.

And I knew the time had come for explanations.

TWENTY

Arizona Caves

Year 45 A.E.

Same Day

Once we were all seated in the main room, Mother and I squished onto the largest of our three seats. Grandad took the lead and I knew that would make things harder.

He would be much more difficult to lie to. He would know I was holding something back; he'd been trained for it. And, as a guard, he would be the most dangerous one to spill any of my secrets to, even if they were just suspicions.

"So we know your class came in as planned this afternoon. We know about Anna. We know your class was taken to a meeting as soon as you came in this afternoon. We know something happened this evening, but. . ." He paused there and gestured at me.

I knew what I had looked like when I left the infirmary, but I had no idea how much worse I might look now. Since it was getting really hard to see clearly out of my right eye, I could imagine it looked a lot worse and I knew I was feeling worse.

My bruises were probably turning all sorts of interesting colors, too. "And then you come in here, hours later, looking like this. . ."

Mom broke in before Grandad could say anything else. "Before you say anything, tell us who did this to you. Was it the same group that has been attacking your friends? Did they catch them this time?"

It was risky, but I decided I would answer Mother first. It felt like the more logical choice. "It was not the same group, and I'm sorry to say they have not been caught."

"Then, who. . ."

"The guards."

Grandfather surprised me then, jumping to his feet, nearly knocking his chair over in his haste. "The guards attacked you!"

I stood then, and though it was difficult, I pitched my voice above his and spoke again. "It wasn't like that. They didn't attack us."

"Us? Who else were you with when this happened?" I had a moment to be thankful that Grandad had at least lowered his voice before speaking this time, before the horror of seeing Jordan and the pain of being too late to help him crashed in on me, nearly overwhelming me.

My next words were spoken in small pieces as I struggled and I choked my way through the tears that rushed out with the words.

"Jordan. . . he. . . we found him. . . it was. . . too late. . . The guards. . . they didn't mean to. . ."

Someone's arms—probably Mother's—wrapped gently around me as my tears changed into broken sobs, but a moment later, I was pushing my way out of her embrace.

The combination of my crying, the long walk back to our unit, and everyone squeezing me tightly must have overloaded my control over the nausea because the next thing I knew, I was running for the disposal area next to our cooktop.

I vaguely felt someone beside me, moving my hair out of the way and smoothing a hand down my back as the sickness overtook me.

Once the wretched heaving finally subsided, Grandad carried me very gently to my own bed, laying me down as cautiously as possible.

"I'm so sorry, love. We should have been more careful with you from the beginning. You must have bruises everywhere." Mother spoke quietly from somewhere beside me.

I wanted to look for her, but didn't dare. The nausea was still there, but with nothing else in my stomach at the moment, it had stopped. However, I knew the wrong movement would bring it out again. . . empty stomach or not.

"And a concussion, if I had to hazard a guess." That voice sounded like Grandmother, but she was further away. As if she was still in the hallway.

"So, no one knew anything about where she was most of the afternoon. And then she shows up here with no security escort, with a concussion and bruises everywhere."

Grandmother spoke up then and her voice grew louder as she spoke. She must be coming into the room now. "There were three boys with her when she opened the hatch. Two of them looked as bad or worse than she did."

Grandad made a noise in response, a sort of grunt. I could tell he wasn't satisfied with that. . . not in the least.

"With all of the attacks going on lately, I'm just so glad to see you're home and—well, not exactly fine—but in one piece."

"Well I guess now is as good a time as any for you to quit that class." I opened my mouth to tell Mother that I couldn't, but I couldn't get the words out. My throat completely closed up.

Had it really only been this afternoon that I had found out Anna was gone, killed? And Jordan—he was gone now, too. And Sophia was in the infirmary, fighting for her life.

Jude, Malcolm and I had been beaten half to death by the guards. How could I stay after all of that?

But leaving won't exactly help, either.

Thinking of what had happened to Anna, I knew it wouldn't do me any good to leave the class. It might even hasten an attack. At least if I stayed, I would have the others grouping with me in the halls and common areas.

"You are going to quit, Eve? Surely—after what's happened?" She was gripping my hand so tightly, I wanted to cry out, but I knew it would just hurt her feelings so I poured the hurt into my voice when I answered her.

As sick as I felt, as much as I hurt, I forced myself into a sitting position before answering.

"I can't. It would probably mean death for me that much faster." At their horrified looks, I hurried on.

"Anna quit. She went on to her internship and it didn't stop them. It might have even given them more of an opportunity. We've been going everywhere in groups for weeks now. But she thought. . . we all thought she would be safe once she wasn't in the class anymore. But she wasn't."

I waited for my words to sink in, for them to understand, but no one gave any sign that they did, so I went on.

"Don't you see I have to stay in the class? I have to stick with them. If I don't, I'm dead for sure."

I know I was harder to understand as I went, because I was crying harder and harder as I talked—as Anna's death. . . and Jordan's crashed in on me again.

"Oh Eve, honey, we didn't know." Mom wrapped me into her arms again and we rocked back and forth slowly as I cried, which—miraculously—did not make me nauseous.

I had cried over Anna earlier, and then again a few minutes ago, but now I cried over Jordan and Sophia and even Jude and Malcolm. I let Mom hold me and rock me and I could feel her stroking my hair and it was so nice, I wanted to stay just like that forever. But I heard Grandad clear his throat and I knew my time was already up.

"Eve, you have to tell us more. I know it's been a rough day, but you have to explain some of what you just said. What about the girl who was in the infirmary? Your classmates said she was attacked. Had she quit, too?"

It took me another minute to compose myself enough to answer him, but I knew he was right. I had to explain some of it. I was just hopeful the tears and my being upset would cover enough of what I couldn't explain.

"She had not quit, but the attackers must have surprised them. It was just Sophia and Jordan in the hall. They must have thought two would be enough. . ." I shrugged before continuing, trying to keep my answers vague.

The last thing I wanted to do was give away anything about Jordan and Sophia's relationship. She did not need trouble on top of what she was already going through.

"The rest of us were sitting in the square talking when she came running out of the hallway, screaming. Adam scooped her up and took her to the infirmary and we went to see if we could help Jordan." At that point, Grandmother interrupted.

"Are you saying you went to where you knew the attackers were?" Mom was squeezing my hand again.

"There were three of us. And we couldn't just leave him." I purposely left out the part about staying in the square and Jude telling me it wouldn't be safe for me to be there alone. I didn't even want to think about how right he was and I certainly didn't want to have to tell my grandmother that I had almost left myself wide open for something so stupid.

"Besides, they were long gone when we got there."

Mother was the one who interrupted this time. "Then what happened to you? How did the guards get involved? Don't tell me this was all just a mistake."

"That is exactly what it was, Mom. We were there in the hall. They came to where the attack happened and we were there. Something had happened to the lights in that hall. The guards couldn't see what was going on until they were right on us."

I looked up at Grandad then, expecting him to defend the guards, but he said nothing so I went on. "I'm sure they were just reacting to Jordan's body. And the three of us were standing while he was laying there. I'm sure that looked really bad to them."

"The other boy—is he?"

I could only shake my head gently to answer her.

In response, both Mom's and Grandmother's hands flew up to cover their mouths.

As they gasped, I forced myself to press on. "I'm sure they thought they had caught the ones responsible. They had no idea we were there trying to help him and I guess they got a little. . . over-zealous in their arrest."

I said each word a little slower as the sentence strung out and I shrugged when I got to the end of the sentence, like I was just repeating what I'd been told.

"Honestly, I don't really remember much of it. I must have hit my head when I hit the ground and the next thing I knew, I was waking up in the infirmary."

Mother started to argue, but I broke in quickly.

“Not the regular infirmary. I think it may be the one the chancellor's people use because it was in that section of the compound and it wasn't nearly as big as the regular one. Not very busy either.” I added, trying to add a little levity.

It was a long time before Grandad convinced Grandmother to leave my side and get some sleep. Mother would not be moved.

She pulled a chair to my bedside and planted herself, shaking her head and plopping in the chair when Grandad tried to reason with her, arguing that she would be more comfortable in her own bed.

“I'll be more comfortable right here where I can see Eve. Besides, she needs someone to watch over her tonight, at least. She has a concussion. She'll need to be checked on throughout the night.”

After several more minutes, Grandad conceded defeat and dropped a gently kiss on my forehead.

“You get some rest, kiddo. You're going to need it.”

I know I mumbled something, but exhaustion was already trying to drag me under the blissful cloak of sleep.

TWENTY-ONE

Arizona Caves

Year 45 A.E.

Day 167

I was so tired of being stuck inside. My plans had not worked out at all like I had expected. Jude and Malcolm were just as stuck, so it wasn't like it was just me, but it sure was frustrating.

My Grandfather had gone over our heads and talked to several of his buddies—including one who was over an entire section of the security. Now all three of us had an armed escort wherever we went.

"Just until you're healing and you can rejoin your class." He'd told me.

But we *were* back in class. We had been back for two days and the guards were still there. They walked us to class and then back to our sections each evening. They didn't talk to us, or make any comments about where we went or what we did—they just followed us everywhere.

Jude and I hadn't so much as touched in four days, because we didn't want any of the guards reporting it back to anyone. I found it more than a little ironic how annoyed I was with it, too.

Five days ago, I had almost decided I never wanted Jude to touch me again. Then we found out Anna had died and suddenly life seemed so much more fragile than I had ever thought. Things like the age difference between us seemed like such a silly thing to worry about.

I decided I didn't mind him holding onto me. . . or following me. . . or holding my hand. . . or kissing me—especially kissing me.

And now I can't even touch him.

It made me want to scream.

And. . . because we were being escorted everywhere we went, we had to be very careful of everything we said and did—not to mention everyone we talked to. The rest of the students barely spoke to us now. They wouldn't sit with us and discuss their plans anymore.

Not that we blamed them; the last thing any of us needed was to have a guard go report to someone that we were planning to hunt down the people who had been attacking us.

For the time being, we made it a point not to linger after class to talk to the others. We even tried to avoid them as much as possible when we saw them huddled together in the halls or the main square. We knew they were talking about their plans, and we knew it would just annoy them if they had to stop because one of us walked over. But it was tough being excluded.

One of the reasons we had refused protection was that we didn't want someone tagging along behind us all the time. Now we were stuck with it anyway.

The only bright side was how well Sophia was doing. After a few days, her family had come to take her back to their living quarters. She'd had it pretty rough initially, but she was doing much better now, except from a psychological perspective.

She wouldn't talk to anyone, not even her own family. She just sat on her bed, facing the wall, and cried. At least we didn't have to worry that she wouldn't be safe. She had guards, too.

Of course, they spent most of their time sitting in her family's main living area, since Sophia wouldn't leave her room. Her parents had finally allowed me to see her. I told her about how Jordan asked about her when we got to him, that his last thoughts were of her. She'd still been in the infirmary then and she had collapsed into my arms, crying hysterically.

I wasn't sure if it was a good thing or not, but when I had looked over at Jude, he'd nodded at me. Then he leaned in and whispered to me, telling me that was the first response anyone had gotten from her.

That was the one thing I did every day, guards or not. I went to visit and spend time with Sophia. Each time, I tried to get another response from her, but all she ever did was sit on her bed and cry.

Her mother told me that sometimes she cried and sometimes she just sat there, but that she never spoke to anyone. I wanted to say something to her mother that might reassure her, but I couldn't think of a single thing. I didn't want to say something that wasn't true, so I told her I'd be back to visit the next day.

Every visit seemed to wear me down. I didn't know what to say to Sophia, so I just rambled on about what was going on in class and around the complex. I ranted a little that we weren't allowed to go out until our injuries healed a lot more, but she didn't acknowledge that any more than she did anything else.

In class, we hadn't been allowed to do much of anything until we healed quite a lot more and that did not sit well with any of us. The others had been out hunting twice without us and we were all pretty miserable about it until Sierra remarked, rather sourly, that they didn't do half as well without us as they would have done with us. It made me feel a lot better and it seemed so make Jude and Malcolm feel better, when I relayed it to them after class.

I discovered during those few days that I did not enjoy sitting on the sidelines, watching. I wanted to be right in the middle of it all. I was frustrated and annoyed when I had to sit in class and watch everyone else practice and exercise and learn new things.

I worried about falling behind everyone else. We were hurt, but we weren't dead. We should be able to participate.

When the attacks had started and other students were being attacked, I didn't remember any of them having to sit on the sidelines, waiting. I asked the instructor about it after class one day. I could tell right away that he didn't want to answer me. I had to push. Finally, I got an answer, but not one I wanted.

“I really think you three just need to take it easy for a few more days. The infirmary will give me the OK when you're up to it.” That was the first answer I got.

“But we're less injured than everyone else who got hurt in the first round of attacks and they were participating in the very next class.” To that, he had nothing to say.

"So, is this something different? Does this have anything to do with the extra security or is it something about *how* we got hurt?" His lack of response was all I needed to know that I had it figured out. Now I just had to figure out who was pulling the strings.

While I was busy trying to figure out who was responsible for driving us all crazy, I kept working to get us cleared for normal duties, so we could get back into class, and away from the security that was dogging our heels and making us all nuts.

So we drove the people in the infirmary crazy. We showed up there every day, insisting they check us out.

And every day we heard the same thing; we weren't ready yet, but they were sure we just needed a few more days. Jude was probably the biggest hold-up, but Malcolm and I were trying to be supportive.

Jude's injuries had been the most severe and the crutches were a huge annoyance for him. He didn't want to use them, but at least he was smart enough to know that using them would help him heal faster.

A side benefit of our frequent trips to the infirmary might have been that our guards weren't allowed in, but we weren't about to mention it to anyone. They weren't very happy about having to wait outside the hatch to the infirmary, but there wasn't anything they could do about it.

And we had the added benefit of a few minutes without them hovering over us.

Not that it gave Jude or me the chance to be alone together—or to hold hands, as we were usually seated on hospital beds spaced at least six feet apart. Still, it was nice to be able to feel like I could breathe without someone looking over my shoulder. And we used that time to share with each other anything that wasn't safe to mention around the guards.

Jude had actually been slipped a note one day in class. He told us about it while we sat there, waiting for our test results. Apparently the other students had set a little trap for the attackers, but it had backfired.

They had all held onto their comms after the latest hunting trip and worked out a little plan.

Adam had been the bait. . . he'd walked around the hallways by himself for almost an hour with the gang listening in on their comms, while they stayed just a hall or two behind him.

Just when they were about ready to give up, he'd been jumped. The others had only been about twenty feet away, but somehow the attackers had heard them and ran away. Adam even managed to trip one of them as they fled, but the others gathered him up and rushed off before they could get caught.

The three of us looked at each other for about ten seconds before we busted out laughing. Clearly we had all seen the same crazy image in our heads. I know the image that came to mind for me was something similar to a silly show that was put on every year for the little kids at the Summer Solstice Celebration.

It was really just a bunch of guys on a little stage, with silly painted faces, falling all over each other.

I didn't remember seeing it much when I was a young child; Mother said we only had one or two Summer Solstice Celebrations at the time, because of how tough some of the winters had been. But they must have had quite a few really good winters in recent years, because there had been a pretty terrific Celebration for the past five years, at least.

I could remember seeing the silly show several times during the past few years.

Once we all stopped laughing and settled down, we talked as quietly as we could about what we could do to ditch the security. We wanted back in on the planning of these things.

Even if we didn't agree with our classmates, we didn't want them getting hurt because they were in a hurry to catch those who were responsible.

We didn't want to continue being left out of the hunting or the training, either. And we certainly didn't want to be so far behind that we actually flunked the class.

It didn't matter that we had actually been beat up by the guards. It would feel like the attackers had gotten the best of us. And they had already taken two of our classmates; our dignity was something we weren't letting them take.

As it turned out, we really didn't need to worry about plotting on our own. We might never know if the staff had just gotten sick of dealing with us, or if the instructor had pushed for us, or if whoever was pulling the strings on our security detail ran out of steam, but the nurse came back to us that very evening to let us know that we were cleared.

"You will need to take it easy in your class. No strenuous or dangerous activity for two more weeks—and you will need to have special first-aid if you go outside for anything." And she handed us each a long rolled-up printout.

I looked at the roll in my hand. Paper was one of the things that were considered rare. We didn't use it unless we had to. It didn't make sense that she would print out something for each of us—for all three of us. It must be something important. I started to unroll mine, but she stopped me.

"Open that later, when you're back in your unit. Your security will escort you there for the evening, but after that, you're on your own." She said it like it was a warning, but all I could think was how exciting it was. I wanted to jump up and down and shout for joy.

No more security dogging my steps, watching every move I made and taking note of every person I talked to. It sounded great to me. And I could tell Jude and Malcolm felt the same way.

Walking back to our units was probably the most exciting thing we had done in days, but for some reason, we were all dragging our feet. I had no idea why. We should all be excited to get back into the swing of things and to be rid of the guards; it was all we had been talking about for days. But, for some reason, we were taking our sweet time getting back to our units.

Jude and Malcolm insisted on walking me to mine first. They did it every night, so it was nothing different, but I found myself reluctant to say good night at the hatch.

TWENTY-TWO

Arizona Caves

Year 45 A.E.

Day 170

We couldn't have been more excited when we walked into the classroom to find everyone gearing up for sparring. We had missed so much of class. Now we could jump right back into the training.

All the time we'd been walking around with security dogging our heels, we were forbidden to use the exercise area. There had been very little we could do on days when the class went outside.

I hadn't wanted to fall too far behind, so I'd taken time in the evenings to do what few exercises I could in the tiny space that was mine. On a lot of days, when the class was outside, we had ended up back in our units, so I had taken advantage of everyone else being away, to do more exercises in the larger living area.

I felt really good about that decision when we started sparring. My first partner was Sierra. It seemed like she was going easy on me at first, but after a few minutes, she figured out that I really didn't need her to go easy on me, so she really came at me.

“I thought you were wounded. Figured you'd be an easy target today, at least.” She laughed as she said it.

I smiled because I knew just how competitive she could be. She got really serious after that. I was thrilled. It was great to be able to *really* use some of the muscles that had needed a good workout for several days. I felt a little smug about not being an easy target.

Jude had obviously been doing the same thing, or else he was in really good shape. A few days had not taken a toll on him because he surprised Jake, and Alan, too, when they took their turns.

Malcolm, however, had either not thought to exercise or his cracked ribs held him back from doing the really strenuous exercises Jude and I had been keeping up.

Adam was his first opponent; that was a tough one for two different reasons. He had never really beaten Adam before—and it didn't look like Adam was taking it easy on Malcolm even a little bit. Malcolm looked like he was really stiff and out of practice.

I felt bad for him; he'd gotten several cracked ribs out of the encounter with the guards and I was sure they would be hurting him later, if they weren't already.

It was tempting later on when I was paired with Adam, to take a little of my frustrations out on him. I told myself it would double as a little payback for Malcolm, since he really wasn't able to do it himself. But, in the end, I played fair.

I actually did get in a pretty good hit when I surprised him. He left himself wide open for it and it was perfectly fair. He was just standing there, with his mouth hanging open, and I couldn't resist.

I was sure he had not left himself open on purpose, especially after watching him with Malcolm. But it was all I could not to fall over laughing at the look on his face when I surprised him.

After that, the fight was pretty boring. We sparred for the rest of our time, but no one landed any more hits. And then we moved on to our next partner.

That was when things got interesting for me because my next partner was Jude. I hadn't sparred with him since long before all the confusing feelings had started popping up between us. And I knew this would be tricky.

Right away I could tell he was going to go easy on me. I wanted to blame it on his injuries, but I'd just watched him take on Alan, and his injuries had not been a problem for him there, so I knew exactly what he was doing, and I knew it had to stop.

I tried teasing him. . . I tried taunting him. . . and then I tried surprising him. If he hadn't been going easy, it would never have worked the way it did. But he *was* going easy and it worked, just not the way I planned it.

I rushed forward, he moved to defend and I hooked a foot under his to send us both tumbling. We landed in a heap, but he wrapped his arms around me and rolled at the last second, so that I ended up on top of him.

I lay there, sprawled over his chest, breathing just as heavily as him, and not able to take my eyes off his.

And once more, we were interrupted.

There were laughs and snickers as the instructor stepped in to pull me off Jude. He made a big production of it, like I had been beating up on a wounded man and I should give it a rest. I knew he'd been right to step in, but I couldn't help but feel a little put out. Again.

We worked our way through the rest of class. The instructor

was kind enough to go over everything the rest of them had actually been learning. He disguised it as a review for the hunting trip scheduled for the next day, but I was grateful, whether it really was or not.

No matter how many times I had seen the class go over the same stuff, most of the things we learned couldn't be learned by watching. We needed to actually do it to really get it. And since we would be hunting on our own for the first time the next day, we needed the practice.

It was after class, though, that I really got into hot water. Jude walked me to my hatch again and I was grateful for it. Even though the guards had been getting on my nerves, I was very aware of how exposed I felt without them. So when Jude offered to walk with me, I didn't even hesitate.

When we got to my unit, I invited him in. He had never met any of my family and I felt oddly compelled to introduce them, especially since my grandmother had seen us together the night I'd come in at 2 A.M. all beat up.

He didn't even hesitate, just followed me through the hatch, which surprised me. I was just as surprised as he to find that no one was there.

Looking at the board by the doorway, I saw that no one was scheduled to be back for several hours.

I hadn't been thinking of my change in schedule.

Usually we were working out with the rest of the class right about now. But lately we had gotten into the habit of coming back to our units after class, because we hadn't been allowed into the workout areas.

I turned to say something to Jude and he was closer than I expected, so I bumped solidly into his chest. I threw up my hands to steady myself and opened my mouth to apologize, but the words stuck in my throat when I looked up at him.

There was a strange look on his face. I watched his eyes as he looked at me and then as his eyes lowered a little.

Was he looking at my mouth?

I found myself looking at his mouth and was suddenly aware that his face was only inches away from me. I was pressed right up against his chest and he reached up to catch my hands in his. He was holding them lightly, but I could feel every single point of contact as if it were on fire.

I looked back up into his eyes. There was a light in them that I had never seen before; it was almost like a reflection of flames. I felt like there were flames licking at my lips, and where I was pressed up against him, it felt hot and tingly. My lips felt almost like they *were* flames.

I felt like I couldn't breathe, like there were tight bands around my chest and they were squeezing. I couldn't seem to look away and then I felt his breath puff out and brush against my skin.

"Not this time."

That was all he said before he leaned in to me and touched his lips to mine.

It was innocent. . . or it should have been anyway. . . but it certainly didn't feel innocent after a second or two.

It felt like I had taken hold of a live wire. There was such a strange electricity everywhere our bodies were touching, everywhere his skin brushed mine, but especially on our lips.

It felt almost like those flames were licking across my lips, not in a bad way or a painful way, but in a way that made me certain that this moment would forever change me. I would never be entirely innocent again. I would forever have this experience to remember. . . to compare. . . to treasure.

And I completely lost track of time. It felt like we stood there forever, but it also felt like it had only been a moment when we broke apart, nearly gasping for air.

He still held my hands in his, but he eased back carefully, and as our bodies separated, I felt suddenly cold. The shock of it was almost as if someone had emptied a bucket of freezing water over us.

I stepped back, somewhat in shock, but I left my hands linked with his. As long as there was a connection, I could hold onto that feeling a little longer.

I knew we couldn't keep doing what we had been doing. It would be a very bad idea. It could get both of us into a lot of trouble. But the temptation to press myself against him, to forget all about the rules, was so strong it was difficult to ignore.

"We should get out of here."

His voice sounded very rough. I was glad to know that he'd been just as affected by what just happened as I was. And I knew he was right, but the last thing I wanted to do was listen to reason. Daringly, recklessly, I stepped in closer to him again.

He backed up and I followed.

"What if I don't want to get out of here?" I teased.

At that moment, our backward journey stopped as Jude bumped into the wall behind him. His mouth dropped open in shock.

I couldn't believe what I was doing, but I knew I did not want to stop. I wanted to push him into kissing me again. I didn't want to be crazy. I didn't want to break any rules. I just wanted to feel that fire again. I looked up at him; I knew he did, too He was just afraid to give in to it.

"Just one little kiss?" I said slowly, trying hard to sound like I'd heard Sophia's voice sometimes when she was teasing Jordan.

At the time, I didn't have a clue what she was doing, but I understood it now.

"I don't think that's such a good idea." And the nerves in Jude's voice gave me the strength to go on.

"What if I do?" I walked the fingers of my right hand up his chest as I said it. He looked down at my hand and I could see him swallow as he did.

That gave me the strength I needed to do the next crazy thing, the most daring thing yet.

I rose up on my toes and nipped lightly at his bottom lip. I had no idea where the idea had come from. I just knew it had taken a lot of courage to do it. Courage seemed to be coursing through me now, so I nipped once, twice and then I really couldn't breathe.

He spun me around so fast, the room blurred around me. And suddenly my back was up against the wall and he was kissing me again. I wanted to savor every single moment of it, but the thoughts in my head got all jumbled up, and all I could do was *feel* as he kissed me.

I felt his hands holding mine between our bodies, and then he was pulling my hands apart and putting his hands on the wall on either side of my head as he continued to kiss me senseless. And then I gasped in surprise when his mouth moved, and he began nibbling the underside of my jaw, along the side of my neck and up to my ear.

I nearly jumped out of my skin at the shock that ran through me when his breath hit my ear.

"You're playing with fire." the words were whispered loudly in my ear, but I wasn't paying attention to them. I was paying attention to the sensations that were rushing through my body.

He was right—I was playing with fire! The fire was raging through me—racing along every limb and over every inch of my skin.

In all the confusion, I didn't even notice for a second or two that he had stopped kissing me. He dropped his head and leaned his forehead against mine. He still held my hands against the wall on either side of my head, but he'd eased his body away gently from mine. We both stood there, panting. The breaths were coming fast and hard from both of us.

"We really need to get out of here. This is not a good idea and you know it."

There was no venom in his voice and I was grateful for that. He had every right to be angry with me. I had pushed him, and if he didn't possess more self-control than I did, we would be in a lot of trouble right now.

It was almost a minute before I could answer. And I tried to sound repentant, I really did, but it came out smug and I couldn't find it in myself to feel badly about that.

"I know." And he looked at me again. The fire was still there in his eyes, so I felt better. It wasn't just me. I was not the only one affected by it all. That was a tremendous relief for me.

"We could go down to the workout area. Pour all this frustration and tension into a good. . . workout." I wasn't sure why I put such an emphasis on the last two words, but when I saw the look on his face and felt the tightening in his gut, I realized it must have been the same thing that had made me nip at his lip.

"Yeah, that sounds like a plan," he said, after a few seconds.

Then he ducked in for a quick, hard kiss before he took my hands and pulled me toward the hatch. We were in the hall and halfway to the main junction before I even realized it. And all the way there, I was smiling.

I was surprised again, when we reached the hallway to the workout room. There was a small alcove just before we reached the doorway to the room. I only knew about it because I'd heard a giggle once as I passed, and I had followed the hall around to find out where it had come from.

Sophia had been there with Jordan.

I expected it to bother me when I realized where Jude was pulling me, but the thought fell out of my head when we turned the corner.

The alcove was created by the placement of an irregular corner and a lack of proper lighting. I was suddenly grateful to whoever was responsible for it, and thrilled that Jude knew about it. I started to wonder about how he might have discovered it, but I didn't get very far because he pulled me into the darkness and then tugged me against him in the dark.

I stretched up on my toes as Jude wrapped his arms around me and leaned in until our lips met. The burn started again—every spot our skin was touching. I felt like every nerve in my body was on fire.

Just like before, time seemed to stop, and at the same time, it stretched out endlessly while Jude's lips roamed over mine. He didn't move down to my neck or around to my ear this time. He just kept moving his lips with mine.

All at once, I felt his mouth open and his tongue licked and rubbed against my lips. Without thinking, I opened my mouth to him and our tongues began a ritual dance together.

I was surprised to hear something like a growl coming from Jude as he spun me around and pressed me up against the hard wall. His hands moved then, roaming possessively down my arms and then back up to brace on either side of my head again. Then he stopped kissing me and dropped his forehead down to touch mine.

"This is so not a good idea." The words came out with little puffs of air because his breathing was just as ragged as mine.

I didn't even have to think of what to say. The words just seemed to trip off my tongue. "Seems like a great idea to me." And I reached up to nip at his lip again.

Just as I did, I heard the growling sound again coming from him and I laughed, because I realized it was his way of telling me I was getting to him.

I felt light-headed at the thought. I'd never considered "getting to" anyone before, especially not someone who was older than me. The whole idea of a mate had always seemed so far off in the future. And I had always had more important things to worry about. I had never given boys much thought—before now.

I hadn't given Jude much thought, either, until we had found out that Anna was dead, and then we both almost died. After that, it had felt important—even urgent—to explore whatever there was between us, before it might be too late.

"We've got to go work out." And he was pulling me along toward the hatch. He stopped right before we went through the doorway and looked me over.

"You really must get that goofy grin off your face—or everyone will know exactly what we have been up to." He yanked me against him for just a second and planted a very quick kiss on my lips, squeezing hard for a moment before loosening his grip.

Then he dropped me back on my feet and pointed a finger at me, which I nipped at playfully. I laughed at him. I couldn't believe how different I felt right this minute.

Not even a day ago, I had been sad and upset and even a little angry. Now I felt playful and silly and absolutely terrific.

He shook his head at me, but there was a grin tugging at the corners of his mouth. He took my hand and we went through the hatch to the workout room together.

No one even looked up when we walked in, but I felt like I had a big sign over my head, announcing exactly what I had been up to all afternoon, and I didn't care a bit who saw it.

We turned toward the locker room to change our clothes. I caught sight of myself in one of the large mirrors on the wall and I could hardly believe it was me.

I had never thought of myself as pretty. Looks weren't really something we thought about much, but I could remember my father calling me his pretty girl when I was younger. And now I could see why, as I stood there, looking at my face.

My cheeks were slightly flushed and my eyes looked very bright, with a different expression than I was used to—a new awareness. My lips were a deeper shade of red and they looked softer and puffier than I remembered them being. I thought the whole effect made me look much older than seventeen.

No wonder Sophia and Jordan had snuck off all the time. If this was a part of the benefits of a romance, I was all for it. I liked it and I felt more grown-up than I had in a long time. It was wonderful and I couldn't wait to kiss Jude again.

I wanted to pull him back out into the hall right that second, but I knew he would just tell me we needed to work out, to get back in shape for class. I blew out a breath, and pushed back the hair that had drifted down over my face.

He would probably be right, too. We were going out on our own in the morning; we needed all the extra workout time we could get. So I quickly got into my workout clothes.

Almost everyone in the class was there working out, including Malcolm. I walked over to him first to check on him. With every lift of the large weights he was holding, he made a grimace of pain. It made me worry about his ribs. I hoped we hadn't rushed to get back into things.

The last thing Malcolm needed was to be back in the infirmary, because we hadn't really been ready to leave it in the first place.

"Hey Malcolm, you doing OK?" I waited for him to stop. After he set the weights back down, I stepped forward and put a hand on his shoulder. He shook his head a little before looking up at me.

"Yeah, I'm good. Just hate that I'm so out of shape. It's tough after all the hard work to suddenly be so weak again."

He looked over my shoulder at someone behind me, and his lips thinned out, as he gritted his teeth. Then he switched hands, picked up the weights and started again.

I knew I wouldn't convince him to stop, so I thought it was best to leave him alone.

Distraction could be a very bad thing for him right now.

I turned and saw Jude come out of the boys' locker room. It felt like the temperature in the workout room went up about ten degrees. He was wearing a pair of pants that were very loose, but the shirt was just tight enough to show off every single muscle.

I remembered—very clearly—being pressed up against those muscles and I remembered what it felt like to have them pressing me against the wall. I had to fan a hand in front of my face and then I realized that what I really needed to do was cool down.

Maybe I should go for a swim. That sounded like the best idea, so I headed for the lap pool.

It was rare in the outdoors to run into actual running water, but it did happen, so anyone who went outside was required to know how to swim.

I was fortunate there as well, because Grandad had taught me as a child. I hadn't been the only one who already knew how to swim, but I was the only one who enjoyed swimming as an exercise.

Most of the class went to the pool after their workout to cool off and relax their tired muscles. I usually went before I got hot or tired and swam laps, but today I was going at least in part to cool off.

I stripped down to my swimsuit and dove in. The cool water immediately helped lower my temperature and I decided to go ahead and get my laps in.

As I swam, I thought about the day. I tried to keep my mind on what we had learned in class and going out to hunt all alone the next day, but no matter how hard I tried, my mind kept going back to the feverish kissing that had gone on in my unit and later in the little alcove just outside the workout area.

When my mind turned to those thoughts, the water didn't feel so cool anymore. I came up for air at the far end of the pool and looked up at the crouched form just at the edge of the pool.

“How long have you been watching me?” I asked, sputtering a

little when my hand slipped off the edge.

"Not long, just a lap or two. You have good form." There was a look in his eye that told me he had been thinking the same things I had been.

For some reason, I was annoyed with him suddenly and I dove under and pushed off, swimming underwater for nearly half the length of the pool before coming back up.

I didn't hear the splash, but I did hear his hands slicing through the water in the lane beside me, when I came up for air.

He was easily keeping pace with me and when I looked over at him, he was grinning. Then he went back under for the next stroke and I was sputtering again as I tried to get back into my rhythm.

I expected him to shoot past me, but the next time I looked at him, he was right in line with me—matching my stride. We swam like that for awhile and I lost count of my laps. It felt like a long time before I finally felt my muscles begin to protest.

I stopped at the far end of the pool.

We were the only ones in the aquatic center, but it still surprised me when he ducked under the rope barrier between the lanes and kissed me.

I wrapped both arms around him and he snaked one arm around me to hold me up and held us both out of the water with the other, as he kissed me with a passion I had never known before.

Our bodies brushed and bumped with the gentle waves that rippled through the pool and our tongues were dancing together again.

I knew what was coming next—and I wanted to be irritated with him. He always stopped each time, just after we'd gotten started.

He had insisted we needed to get out of my empty unit and be where there were other people.

He had pulled me along with him to the workout center.

I had come in here to cool off and here he was again—kissing me with such passion, I was surprised the water around us wasn't boiling.

"How long did you say your unit will be empty?"

I felt my mouth drop open in shock. And then he was laughing, probably at the look on my face.

"Do not worry, Eve. I am not serious." He pulled himself out of the water and reached a hand down to me.

When he pulled me out of the water, our bodies bumped again, but he stepped back and quickly handed me a towel.

“I apologize. I do not intend to send you mixed signals.” And then he did the most unexpected thing. He bent and kissed my hand.

“I will let you get back to your workout and I will get back to mine.” But he just stood there, holding my hand. And I didn't want him to let go any more than he looked like he wanted to let go.

Fortunately, or unfortunately, the door swished open and we heard Adam's voice booming and bouncing off the tile around us.

“Hey guys. How's the water?” He had a towel over his shoulder and he was wet from the shower. I still remembered the first day our class had come in to work out. The instructor had brought us in to introduce the equipment to anyone who was unfamiliar with it. And he had been very firm about the rules, one of which was that you had to shower before you got into the pool if you had been working out.

If you came in and swam before your workout, you could do so without a shower, but only if you were clean. At the time, several of the students had complained about the rule, but they all followed it, and I was grateful for that.

“It's great!” Jude said, as he took my hand and headed for the door.

The rest of our workout was pretty uneventful. We parted ways and I was a little glad of it. It would be really hard to concentrate on my workout with him next to me, distracting me.

He was waiting by the hatch when I walked out of the locker room, showered and dressed. He took my hand as we went through the hatch together.

I realized in that moment that I was just as excited about walking through the hall, holding his hand, as I was when we were kissing. The only difference was the warmth; it was like a warm glow flowing softly through me, instead of a fire raging across my skin. I felt a smile bloom on my face as we walked.

Obviously, he had calmed down quite a bit, too. He didn't even hesitate when we passed the alcove we had ducked into earlier. We walked hand-in-hand through the complex until we reached my unit, and only then did he kiss me again.

This kiss was different, though. It was slow and lazy, with none of the feverish excitement of our earlier kisses. His fingers lightly touched my face as he pulled back slightly. Then he traced my lips lightly with his finger as he eased back a little more.

"I will see you in the morning," and he stepped back, clearly waiting for me to go inside.

I had to swallow before I could say anything. "In the morning. Yes." And I nodded to him, before I turned and stepped through the hatch.

TWENTY-THREE

Arizona Caves

Year 45 A.E.

Day 171

Jude was there in the morning, waiting for me. I stepped out into the corridor and he was there, leaning against the opposite wall.

"How long have you been standing there?"

His smile bloomed slowly in answer. "Long enough." And he pushed off the wall and held out a hand to me. "Do you think you are ready for today?"

It occurred to me then, that we wouldn't be able to be on a team today. We wouldn't be able to sneak off and melt the snow with a few feverish kisses, while everyone else struggled to keep up with us.

He must have seen the change in my features and realized what it was about. He stopped walking, put a finger under my chin and lifted my face.

"We will have time later." And then he touched his lips to the tip of my nose before turning and walking towards the classroom again, tossing over his shoulder as he went, "We are early. There is another dark alcove near the classroom."

That was all I needed. I lengthened my stride and caught up to him easily. Then, when he sped up, I did so as well.

We nearly raced through the complex in our hurry to get to the alcove. We were laughing as we turned the corner and he hurriedly pulled me into the dark alcove—the one I had *not* known about.

Once there, however, his behavior changed completely. There was no hint of speed in any of his actions. His hands were lightly touching either side of my face as he looked into my eyes. I felt almost mesmerized by the look in his eyes.

He wasn't even kissing me and I had already lost track of time. It was an entirely new experience.

When he finally did kiss me, it was slowly—like the kisses at my doorway. His lips were soft against mine and he kept his hands on my face. I couldn't even begin to describe the sensations working their way through me, but I had a feeling I was in danger of losing my heart to him.

Maybe I already have.

I reached up with my own hand and tangled my fingers in his hair as he kissed me. And, without any warning, the kisses changed again.

He spun me around with a growl deep in his throat and pulled me up on my toes as he leaned back against the wall behind him. I felt like I was sprawled out over him. His hands were twisted in my shirt at my waist as he kissed me.

After what seemed like forever, he finally let me go and looked at the digital on his wrist. I heard another growl, but it was a different one than I had heard before. This was one of irritation.

"We must go. Come. We will finish this later."

His eyes held a promise that sent a shiver of anticipation through me.

Despite his concern, we were the first ones to walk into the classroom.

The instructor was there, but we had expected that. He was looking over a list that was clipped to the small board he was fond of carrying. It was almost a minute before he looked up and acknowledged us.

He didn't say anything, just nodded his head and went back to his list. So we headed in to check our gear.

This was it—our final test. I felt sure I would pass. This was where I fit in—finally. I had found my place in the caves.

As we moved closer to the gates, Jude grabbed my hand and pulled me closer to him. He didn't say anything, but he looked nervous.

“I am really not comfortable leaving you to go off alone. We still don’t know who is responsible for all the attacks on our group. What if they take advantage of us being separated?”

After a moment, he added, “This is a mistake, for everyone to go off alone.”

“I don’t think there’s anything we can do. You have to let me go—we have to pass this final test. This is what I want to do—a permanent position. Once we pass the final test, we can hunt together.”

We hadn’t really discussed it, but I was hoping Jude would want to do this permanently. If he didn’t—well, we’d figure something out so we could be together.

"Eve, watch yourself out here. Do not let your guard down for a second. I will let you go," and he let go of my hand as he said it. "But I'll be watching out for you. I'll be somewhere nearby. And I will be waiting for you at the gate when we're done."

He reached for my hand again, squeezed it once before adding, "I'll be waiting. . . for you."

Everyone was being given final instructions about not going too far, and to be back at the gate before dark.

Then one by one, we walked into the forest. I looked back once, to see Jude watching me, and then I took a deep breath —and disappeared into the woods.

I couldn't believe what I was seeing.

Memories ran through my head. Images quickly flew past. Alan, never being with us, when we stuck together in groups, going to and from class. Alan, showing up in the hallway, seconds after the guards slammed me to the ground. I hadn't even realized I'd seen that—one of the negatives of my being slammed to the ground.

There were more. . . Alan slipping out of the room just before they told us about Anna; Alan, who looked like he knew exactly where we were going, when they led us through the crazy maze in the chancellor's area.

Alan's face, as he came over the hill and saw where we were, showing no surprise; but what had looked very much, to me, like anger. Alan in the classes, clearly doing what I was doing —holding back. Why?

This was why.

I was so angry. But I was also smart. I was not about to stumble into anything here and end up dead over this. I stayed exactly where I was and waited, watching. I didn't have to try to figure out what they were doing. I knew exactly what was going on right in front of me.

Alan was some sort of spy, working for the chancellor, feeding him information about people who weren't doing what they were supposed to do.

I thought back to Anna. Had Alan been responsible for that? Had he told the chancellor that we found that city—which we weren't supposed to see?

Did that mean the attacks were not what I thought they were? Did that mean they were killing off our class one by one? The thought almost made me move forward—almost. I wanted to do something, anything, to stop him before he got the rest of us killed.

And then something stopped *me.*

Jude! I knew he was out here, probably close by. He had said he was going to stick close. He could stumble into this scene at any moment. I told myself to calm down, to think. I couldn't protect anyone if I gave myself away right now. I needed to think, to be smart and see what I could see.

Maybe they would move in a minute. Maybe they were almost done. And then I knew it was too late. I heard the voice a second too late.

"Hey Alan, sorry. Didn't know you were out here. I'll just head. . ." but the voice stopped. I could only feel relief that it wasn't Jude.

But Malcolm was my friend. What would they do to him?

Have they already done it?

I couldn't hear anything and he wasn't in my line of sight. I tried to inch forward without making any noise. I knew it would be all over if they heard me—and I knew Alan had amazingly sharp hearing. I'd seen that in action during our training.

And then I saw Malcolm. The man Alan had been talking to had him slung over his shoulder and they were walking toward me.

"No, just get him out of here. We can't risk anyone seeing him." Alan sounded panicked. I could understand that. He was faced with being found out if anyone saw him with this man.

“He's not going to like it.” The man's voice was not at all what I had expected. I had been sure he would sound cruel, rough, and perhaps dimwitted. Instead, he sounded a little stressed, but calm—even pleasant. His voice was smooth, cultured and definitely not dumb.

“It can't be helped.” Alan was sounding more panicked with each word.

“OK, but it's you who will have to deal with him.” And the man sounded worried. Well that made sense. People were usually afraid of someone who wouldn't hesitate to murder whoever who was in their way, even a kid.

“I know. I'll take care of it.” And then I could hear two sets of feet moving. I thought about poor Malcolm. Oh, I hoped he wasn't dead, that there might be some hope for him. I knew that was wishful thinking, but I couldn't help it. I had to have some hope to hold onto.

I knew now just how ruthless the chancellor was. If he could have Anna and Jordan killed, he wouldn't hesitate over Malcolm. . . or me.

I had no idea what I could possibly do to help Malcolm, even if he was still alive. If I came out of hiding, they'd just do the same to me.

So I stayed there, lying in the snow and wishing they would just go away, so I could come out. Finally, the man nodded to

Alan, who walked away, while the unknown man came toward me, still carrying Malcolm.

I looked him over as he moved.

He was big; there was no way I was going to take him out by myself. Even if he had the weight of Malcolm weighing him down, I knew he would drop him in a heartbeat if he needed to.

Which meant I had no hope of helping Malcolm. It was not a comfort to know there was absolutely nothing I could do right now. And I almost wished for Jude. At least he could help me.

The two of us could definitely handle this guy.

But he wasn't coming, no one was. And as much as I wanted the help, I was glad Jude was safe.

The man was walking past me now. He didn't show any sign that he'd seen or heard me, so I moved as silently as I could to follow him. If Malcolm was still alive and the guy was taking him somewhere to dump him, knowing the cold would take care of him, I could wait until he was gone and then wake Malcolm.

If he was already dead or the guy was taking him somewhere to kill him, I had less of a chance to help, but I did have a chance. So I moved along the tiny path I had discovered in the trees and followed the man carrying Malcolm.

If there was any chance that I could help him, I knew I had to do it. I had to try. I hadn't been able to save my father. I hadn't been able to save Anna. I hadn't been able to save Jordan.

I was not giving up easily on Malcolm.

I followed as quietly as I possibly could.

I followed as he wove his way through the trees. I was careful to be as quiet as possible and he never gave any indication that he heard me. I lost track of time, following him and while I did, I thought about other things that had not added up at the time, but made perfect sense now.

I realized now why Alan had never looked even a little bit afraid when we were being attacked left and right. He had known he had nothing to fear. He had known all along that they weren't after him.

And that thought made me very angry.

I wanted to go find Alan and beat the crap out of him.

I wanted to tell him just what a jerk he was. I wanted to find out why it was so important for him to spy on us and relay information back to the stupid chancellor about us. But at the same time, I wanted to do everything I could to help Malcolm. So I continued to follow the man carrying Malcolm.

The next thing I knew the light in the sky was changing. It took me by surprise so much that I nearly walked into a tree, which would have given me away nicely. I looked around me and realized how far we had come.

Would I be able to get back in time? Could I leave Malcolm?

What would happen to him if I was dead? And why was this guy not heading back to the complex?

It took about thirty seconds to decide, which was probably too long. I couldn't help Malcolm if I was dead, I'd already established that. This man was not heading back to the complex and I had no idea where he was going.

If he was going back to the complex, he obviously had another way in, but I wouldn't exactly be able to slip in behind him without being noticed. So I was out of luck either way. My only hope was to get to the complex as fast as I could.

But could I make it?

There was no way to know, but I had to try. I turned around and realized I had already lost sight of the guy. It was one more reason I had to get back to the gate. I was fortunate to have spent so much time in the forest hunting.

I knew so much of it without even having to think. It was practically no time before I recognized where I was. I headed off in the right direction.

It was slow going for a few minutes. This area had gotten some pretty thick snow and I wasn't wearing snowshoes this trip, which I was pretty glad of since they would slow me down later and I needed every second.

I didn't even give a second thought to explaining why I hadn't managed to snag anything in my hunt. I just kept moving toward the gate in the straightest line I could find. Before long I was running.

The muscles in my legs were screaming from over-use, burning with exhaustion. But I knew I couldn't stop, I couldn't rest. To stop or even to slow down would mean death. If I didn't get to the gates in time, I would be locked out.

They didn't wait for anyone. I knew that better than most of the complex.

Memories of watching my father flew past my vision and it distracted me for a moment from the pain in my legs.

I had sat around far too long, recovering after being attacked. If I had been able to work out properly instead of sitting around, I would be faster. Instead, I was trying to pull strength and speed from my legs that they didn't have right now. Still, I pushed my muscles even harder.

When I broke through the edge of the trees, I was breathing so hard, it sounded like thunder in my head. Or maybe that was my heart. I kept pushing my legs faster and I was shocked to find more strength—strength I didn't know I had

Or maybe it was the adrenaline in my system. There had to be adrenaline being pumped throughout my body right now. Fear usually triggered adrenaline, didn't it?

I looked up at the gates and was momentarily distracted by how clear the guard stations were from this vantage. I saw someone step out of one of the towers and my heart jumped into my throat.

Not now, please not today was all I could think. *Why does he have to be on duty right now?* In that moment, I realized I could already hear the sound of the heavy wheels that moved the doors into place.

And I knew I was not going to make it. I was too late, already.

So I stopped.

The memory of watching my father turn away that day was suddenly more clear than it had ever had.

I remembered watching him as he had stopped that day. I had never understood why. It had not made sense to me why he stopped, turned around and went back into the woods.

But I understood now. I knew what was next and I knew what I had to do.

He was still there, looking right back at me, but I could see he had sunk to his knees. It was hard, but I knew I couldn't afford to let loose the tears that were threatening.

Tears were a death sentence out here.

I almost laughed at the irony of that, but then I stopped myself. Laughing wouldn't be a very good idea either. So I looked at him for another moment, the only person who had ever understood me the way my father had and, after a few seconds, I saw the slight nod of his head.

I felt a little bit better then.

He was telling me it was OK, that everything would be OK. So I snapped a jaunty little salute, not right at him, but in the general direction of the gate and then I turned back toward the woods.

At least he would know what had happened. He would tell Mom and Grandmother. At least they wouldn't always wonder. At least they would know. Not that knowing was much better.

For just a second, I thought I could hear my mother crying, just a ghost of the sound I had heard the night my father hadn't made it. It almost undid me, so I shoved those thoughts to the back of my mind and concentrated on moving a little faster.

And then my thoughts took another turn and it was truly a struggle to control my tears.

Jude. Why had I found him now, discovered what we had together, only to lose him. And like this, too. . . *Why like this?* Was there no justice in this world?

My Grandfather wouldn't even know to tell him. Unless Jude came looking for me, and asked them point blank, he would just wonder. Oh, they would get around to putting my name on the board at some point. . . the one that reminded us all how important it was to be inside before the gates closed, but there would be no explanation. . . no reason.

I would never see him again. Never again would I feel the touch of his lips on mine, the feel of my hand in his or the warmth that enveloped me when I was in his arms.

Unless I manage to survive. That thought shocked me, nearly stopped me.

Is that even possible? Could someone really survive out here?

No way. It's not possible. If someone had survived, we would have heard about it. . . wouldn't we?

I thought of the chancellor and I knew immediately that he would have covered something like that up. He would do everything he could in order to make sure we had no idea something like that was possible.

A chill that had nothing to do with the temperature raced down my spine. How far would the chancellor go. . . really?

Would he kill someone to keep his secret?

I was surprised to realize I already knew the answer.

Of course he would. My thoughts turned then to my father and I couldn't help but wonder.

Could he have survived? He had all the extra knowledge Grandad had taught to me as I grew up, so he knew how to survive.

Was it possible? *Could he have survived out here?*

That made no sense though. Where would he have gone? The world was just ice and snow. If he had somehow survived, he would have come back to the caves.

But would he have had a chance? Would he really have tried?

If he had made it through the night. . . and tried to return to the caves. . . surely the chancellor would have found out about it. And I was more sure than ever that the chancellor would have found a way to get rid of him to keep all those crazy secrets from being found out.

Surely Dad would have been smart enough not to come back.

So, what if he had somehow survived. . . and not come back . . . knowing what he did about the chancellor?

Could he have found some way?

Suddenly I was determined to survive, to find out the answers to my questions, to figure out all the things my father had told me about before he disappeared, to find out if there was a chance I could be right.

I was running again. And determination had lent new speed to my legs.

The city. . . was all I could think.

That ruined city was my only chance. And I didn't have much time. I hit the tree line at a run and I didn't slow down. Sunset was coming and darkness was not my friend. Dark would bring much more than just the cold with it. The big animals came out of hiding then—and they would be hunting.

There were other dangers that would come with the darkness, as well. There was a very real danger of falling down a hill or over a cliff.

I would never make it to the city if darkness descended before I had time to get to that open field.

Even making it to that hill where we had first seen it would not be enough. I had to make it down that hill. It was much too steep to maneuver in the dark. And I knew as well as anyone that darkness fell quickly, especially this time of year. So I needed to cover as much ground as I possibly could before it came.

I slowed down only to snag the kill I'd made earlier. In all the craziness, I'd nearly forgotten I'd left it hanging.

I was suddenly thankful it just happened to be in my path.

If I'd had to detour to get it, I would have left it hanging, but it was on the way, so I stopped long enough to cut it down and then I was running toward the hill at full steam again. I could only hope there was enough shelter there for me to survive.

That got me thinking about why people didn't survive outside the complex. Most of them probably had no idea the city was there. And even if they did, they might not be able to get there quickly enough if they missed the gate.

How many people spent precious minutes banging at the gate, pleading with the guards, promising insane things if the guards would just bend the rules and let them in?

Now that I was thinking about it, I realized it did happen a lot more often than would seem possible. Why would so many people be late coming back to the complex? They all knew the consequences; they learned them as soon as they could walk and talk.

So why would anyone ever put themselves in the position to be late and get locked out? That made no sense. The questions rolled around in my head as I ran and brought to mind that early morning that I'd been so certain was a drill.

In the circumstances of punishment, it was very different. The people being punished were not given the opportunity to be late. They were sent out in the middle of the night or right at the time the gate was meant to close for the night.

A shudder ripped through me at that thought.

I remembered all too well, a time when someone had sat down just outside the gate and frozen to death. Their remains had been right in front of the gate in the morning, so that everyone who was there waiting to go out had seen it.

That had been one of the days I happened to be outside the complex, just close enough to see clearly what everyone else saw when the outer gates opened for the morning patrols.

I remembered wondering at the time, why the guards would open the gates if they knew the body was there. But now, knowing what I did about the way things really were, that was an easy answer. They'd done that to remind us all of exactly what waited for us right outside the gates.

Now the memory just made me angry. There was no reason for such behavior, no sense to it. Why couldn't the chancellor just be honest? It wasn't like they had anywhere else to go, not really.

The other cave systems were much too far away to get to before a person froze to death. So they were stuck with the chancellor.

If only the people on the moon base had survived. . .

If the government had gone on the way it was supposed to after that rogue moon had hit Earth. . .

There were so many what-ifs. None of them had any chance of really changing things now, but they were there all the same.

If only the leader whom Grandmother worked for had made it to the caves. . .

That was another thing that had never made sense to me. If Grandmother had been his aide, wouldn't she have come to the caves in the same transport he was in?

Shouldn't he have made it, too? Or had they been in separate transports? That was the only thing that made sense. The thoughts were bouncing around in my head now as I ran, dodging tree limbs and running around tangles of brush.

I had a moment to think it was a good thing the nights had been so cold lately, because the snow was hard and easy to run atop.

I stopped for just a second to get my bearings. I knew I was close now, but I wanted to be sure. The last thing I needed was to get lost in the dark; that was becoming more of a reality every second. The sky was getting darker by the minute.

It was only another second to check the sky before I was moving again—and only a minute or so after that, when I topped the hill and saw the city. It looked like it was still a pretty fair distance, but in the half light of sunset, it was lit up bright, reflecting the sun—I knew I would have no trouble at all finding it in the semi-dark, so I moved down the hill as quickly as I could.

A measure of relief flowed through me, giving me hope that I'd not felt a moment before.

It was a miracle that I'd reached this hill while there was still some light. It was steep and I was sure it could have been treacherous if I wasn't careful. I made my way down as carefully as I could while being cautious. I was surprised when I looked up and realized I was at the bottom.

When I looked at the city again, it was much closer; that bolstered the hope in me. I looked ahead of me and saw several problem areas. The terrain was mostly flat between me and the city, but it was all unfamiliar and I could not afford to trip and get hurt out here in the middle of nowhere.

I had about a second to decide, even though I already knew I needed to use my flashlight. I had hesitated because it was in the bottom of my bag and the time it would take to dig it out would cut into my time to get to the city. But I also knew if I didn't get it out, I might never make it to the city. So I pulled the pack off my back and started digging.

The sound of a twig snapping had me shifting into a fighting stance. In the silence, it was incredibly loud. . . and close. It was a struggle, but I was able to choke back the scream that jumped into my throat. The last thing I needed to do was help the beast who was coming for me.

I nearly shouted with relief when my fingers touched the flashlight. I pulled it out and debated switching it on. I could use it to find my way, but would I be leading someone to me at the same time?

When I heard nothing else for a few seconds, I decided it was worth the risk. I switched it on, pointing it out in front of me and then moving as quickly as I could over the unfamiliar ground.

Fortunately it was mostly flat, so I was able to move quickly. I could only hope that whatever was out there would lose interest and go after something else with me moving away so quickly and not at all afraid of it.

But it wasn't meant to be.

Only seconds later, I heard another noise behind me. It was loud enough to be a large predator so I picked up my pace. I knew the flashlight beam would give me away, but I held onto the hope that it would help more than not. . . especially now that I was moving faster.

The ground beneath my feet was getting more and more slick and it didn't take long to realize I was on a frozen body of water, a lake or river or even a pond.

I nearly panicked before it occurred to me that it could work to my advantage. Animals would be just as ungainly on ice as I would be.

I paid special attention to where I put my feet. In fact, I was paying so much attention to where I put my feet that I didn't hear the sound coming up behind me.

It was not at all like the noise from before. It was more of a scraping and when I heard it, I thought it must be claws on the ice.

I turned to see what was coming up behind me. Whatever it was, I wanted to be as prepared as possible.

But I never got the chance to see what it was. I never got the chance to fight or flee or even see what hit me. I just saw darkness as something hit me from behind. . . hard.

We should have known. . .

We should have expected this.

How can life really go on the same as it always was?

The short and simple truth is—it can't.

Of course it can't.

Life doesn't just. . . go on. . . after a brush with extinction.

We were stupid to think that it would.

That it could. . .

But of course we did—because we're human.

Only human. . .

We should have handled things better.

We should have banded together—learned from the past;

learned to be better neighbors, better stewards, and better humans.

But when has the human race ever learned from our mistakes?

TURN THE PAGE
FOR EXCLUSIVE

BONUS

MATERIAL

DISCUSSION QUESTIONS

WARNING : SPOILERS AHEAD!

If your book club is reading ***Life After E.L.E.*** and would like to chat or skype with me, please contact me via my website: http://jcmorrows.com/contact.

1) If you found yourself in a post-apocalyptic world, how do you think that would affect your faith? Would you hold on tighter to God and His promises – or would you maybe begin to question His plan?

2) Eve does not really exhibit signs of faith in God. Do you think her experience—watching her father be locked out of the compound—might have been easier if she had been able to lean on God?

3) The Bible tells us not to lie. However, given her few disadvantages—like size—do you think Eve was justified in hiding her abilities and skills? Would you have done the same in her position? Do you believe she would have handled things the same way, if she had a strong faith in God, and was actively trying to live her life according to His commandments?

4) Eve's father played an intricate part of the story, even though he was only in the story as a part of his daughter's memories? Do you believe his loss could possibly have been a part of God's plan for the family. . . for Eve? Why or why not?

5) Where do you stand on the issue of hunting what is essentially an endangered—or rather. . . an extinct—animal? Considering that it was about to kill Adam, do you think Eve made the right choice?

6) Human nature is to save oneself, but there are many people who would have attempted to stop the punishment in the beginning—especially that of a group of children? Do you think the lack of response from the people in the compound is due to the early hour, the fear everyone feels for their own lives. . . or possibly that a bit of their humanity has actually been destroyed by their circumstances and living conditions?

7) Every person has a different idea and/or standard for what they consider appropriate in a romantic/physical relationship between teens. Do you feel that Eve and Jude perhaps became a little too involved during the story? Knowing what has happened to Eve, do you think the situation might have been a bit easier on Jude if they had not become so entangled? If you knew you were going to be separated from the one you love—possibly forever—would you allow yourself to become seriously involved or do you think the separation might be easier if you keep your distance?

THANK YOU!

I dedicate this book to everyone who helped me get through that first year of NaNoWriMo; my family, my author friends, and my writing buddies! You may not know it, but ***Life After E.L.E.*** was started the first year I participated. . . *and WON*. . . NaNoWriMo.

My mother was the one who challenged me. Without her, I might never have joined up—and if I had never joined NaNo, *E.L.E.* Might never have emerged from the murky labyrinth of worlds and characters that is my mind.

A huge THANK YOU goes out to my readers, fans, and my wonderful editor who encouraged me to work on *E.L.E.* and get it in shape to be published!

And—though I didn't fit in at all with my home region—there were a few people within the group who inspired me and encouraged me, so thank you! You know who you are!

There is also one; without whom, I would never have been able to do any of this; my Heavenly Father. HE knew what I could do before I was even born and HE has inspired and guided and blessed my writing. And He has blessed me with a miraculous circle of family and friends who see my talent, even when I don't —and encourage me to *just keep writing!*

God Bless you all!

~ JC

ABOUT THE AUTHOR

JC Morrows—best-selling author of Christian YA speculative fiction. . . drinker of coffee and avid reader—is a storyteller in the truest sense of the word.

She finished her first speculative fiction novel purely for the enjoyment of her mother—also known as her biggest fan, but of course she couldn't stop with just one.

JC has been telling stories in one form or another her entire life and once her mother convinced her to write them down. . . well, she couldn't stop.

But she gives God all of the glory for her talent and ability!

"And the LORD answered me, and said, Write the vision, and make it plain upon tables, that he may run that readeth it."

Habakkuk 2:2 KJV

NEWSLETTER SIGN-UP

Do Your Part. . .

If you have a personal blog, please consider featuring JC. If you enjoyed "A Tragic Consequence", please consider rating this book and leaving a review on GoodReads and/ or your favorite retail site. . .

it only takes a sentence or two. . .

Of course, if you love it and you're inclined to write more, feel free. . . and THANK YOU!

www.ingramcontent.com/pod-product-compliance
Lightning Source LLC
Chambersburg PA
CBHW010447310726
48979CB00018B/2842/J

* 9 7 8 1 9 4 8 7 3 3 4 1 0 *